# SANTA'S NAUGHTY BOY

## by

## Wendy Rathbone

**Santa's Naughty Boy**
**Copyright © December 2020 by Wendy Rathbone**
**A publication by: Eye Scry**

TITLE: Santa's Naughty Boy
Author: Wendy Rathbone
Cover by: Wendy Rathbone
ISBN: 978-1-942415-39-8

Address all inquiries to the author at:
wrathbone@juno.com

For  Della
as always


and


Jackie North
most excellent beta reader

# Chapter One

*Angel*

Sleet falls in the black slippery streets, on the front walk, and against the window panes. It leaves behind white slush on the outside sills, stark against the deep onyx of the cold Alaskan night.

People are used to such weather here, especially in November, but this evening seems extra cold and dismal, the kind of night you stay home and slither under a pile of blankets in front of the fireplace, share warmth with your dog or, if you are lucky enough to have one, a lover or a spouse.

From behind the bar, Royal watches me wipe down the two back booths, his gaze hard and unmoving like always. As if he's waiting for me to fuck up and not do it right. Like always.

He's been picking on me more today because it's slow. We're all on edge. I and the other cocktail waiters aren't making much in tips, and Royal's cash register is too empty for his liking. He's all about the money, a no-nonsense sort of guy who keeps a very expensive and spoiled boyfriend on the side.

*Prancer's* is Royal's pride and joy and has made him pretty well-off, but days like these make him more than grumpy. He's already sent Joeybear home, but he refuses to close the bar early. He'll make the rest of us stay until one or two a.m. finding more make-work for us to do like wash invisible spots off glassware, wipe down already sparkling countertops, or clean and re-clean the glass windows of the outer and inner doors of the entrance, and sweep away ice dragged in on the shoes of customers from the enclosed, entry-way alcove.

I always hate that alcove job. It's cold in that little area, and my waiter uniform consists of only black boots, tight leather pants, and a bow tie. It's the holidays, so for the next six weeks the bow tie is red instead of black, and we wear more glitter in our hair than usual, along with metal bracelets of red and green bells.

My bare, flat titties turn to stone nubbins in that alcove, and Royal won't let us wear jackets even while cleaning out there.

"The customers want to see skin, so we'll give them skin," he always says.

Of course he's right. That's the only entryway, and the first thing customers view of this little gay bar in the big woods. They're going to want to see young, toned men with gleaming tans even in the dead of winter, so that's what we give them.

"Angelbaby, don't forget to wipe under the cushions, too," Royal says from across the bar.

When he snaps orders at me in public like that, it makes me feel like nothing. Like I'm meat and a tool, fit only for being ordered around to deliver drinks, flirt, and clean. In truth, it is kind of the job description. And Royal is a fair and just boss. But still!

If I didn't make so much money from tips, especially in spring and summer, I wouldn't be here. But this job pays for my BMW, and a rather nice condo I don't have to share with any sloppy roommates.

There are only two customers in the bar right now. The music is playing a low and sexy background beat to accompany the drunken, lazy way they are leaning into each other as they speak in low voices probably about past hookups, or future ones, or hooking up with each other right now.

They aren't paying any attention to Royal. Or me. But I still feel as if Royal is broadcasting criticism. I feel like he picks on me the most. Probably because I'm the youngest at twenty-two. And, damn it I'll just say it, I'm the fucking cutest waiter here. Because of that, I swear I just play right into the role of Royal's kinky all-the-time need for control.

When I finish bussing the tables, I carry the tub of dirty dishes and rags to the kitchen. Royal stops me at the swinging double doors.

"You spilled crumbs all over. Get the broom and do the job right!"

I nod, holding back a heavy sigh.

"Angelbaby, don't give me that look. Just do the job right and I'll stop having to micromanage you all the time."

I ignore him. He likes to act big. But he's not really all that mean. He gave us all these cute nicknames to go with the job. Joeybear. Bobbykitten. Hennydoll for Henry. Oh how Henry hates it! And me, well, my real name is Angelo. I don't look like an Angelo. Never did. I actually *do* look like an Angelbaby. And this Angelbaby gets the best tips, so I don't mind it at all.

After I rinse the dishrags and put the glassware and appetizer dishes in the dishwasher, which is barely half full—that's how slow it's been around here today—I return to the main bar with the sweeper. It's not really a vacuum cleaner. It runs on wheels, which make the brushes spin, and is great for getting crumbs up from flat, all-weather carpet.

As I walk toward the back booths, the sweeper makes a soft raspy noise as I push it. I do a little dance, balancing the handle and circling it like it's my grind partner, thrusting toward the handle's shaft as I sweep up the crumbs. Out the corner of my eye, I see Royal shake his head and turn away, but not before I note the barest curve of a smile on his lips.

If I do nothing else right tonight, well, at least I've done this to the boss's satisfaction.

Just as I'm bending and gyrating to get the sweeper under the table, I hear the outer alcove door slam shut in the wind and the inner door's bell jangle over the canned beat of the music. A brand new customer enters.

I glance up to see a somewhat burly guy in a red parka lined with white fur enter our gay and friendly establishment. He has on a red knit cap with a long tail that dangles over his shoulder. A cute pom-pom on the end of that cap bounces against his broad chest.

As he walks toward the booth I've just cleaned—hella spotless now, I'm proud to say—he tugs off the parka and underneath reveals a dark red velvet shirt over black trousers, and knee-high black boots that are folded down at the tops. Those are what I call Santa-boots, and immediately I love them on him. And the red velvet? That color brings out a glow in the cheeks.

He pulls off his cap and down tumble brilliant waves of light brown hair streaked with flashes of gold. I sorta want to ask who his stylist is, but we haven't even met yet, and that's kind of a personal question.

Instead, I shove the sweeper toward the back wall, stick out my flat, naked chest, flex my arms a bit, and approach.

"Hi, I'm Angelbaby. It's pretty damn cold out. Can I get you anything to warm you up, Daddy?"

Of course I put in *all* the inflections in *all* the right places. I tilt my head so my smile comes off as sarcastic but still cutely enticing.

He looks up at me with eyes the color of a moonlit sea, dark with just a hint of blue.

"Hmm," he says. His gaze twinkles. I mean, actually twinkles! "I'm not cold but I've been craving a rum and Coke all day."

I sashay off, hoping he's staring at my ass because these leathers hug my slim hips perfectly, and I credit them for at least half of my generous tips.

Royal hands me the drink which I put on a tray. He says, "You know him?"

"No."

Royal purses his lips. "Haven't seen him around before."

"Me, either. But he's cute."

Royal raises an eyebrow. "If you like the burly, older type."

I shrug. "Who doesn't?"

But the guy isn't all that old. Or burly. Broad, yes, with muscle, but trim, like a man who's seen a few battles or a long walk through the ice fighting White Walkers. I'm a *Game of Thrones* fan, so my brain automatically measures guys up by that standard. It's not fair of me, I know, but it's the maze my mind walks.

I set down a round, cardboard coaster with the Prancer's logo on it of a reindeer hopping over a full, yellow moon. I start to place the drink on top but the guy grabs the coaster and stares at it.

He mumbles something that sounds like: "He's a lot thicker in the haunches than this, and the face is too short."

"What?" I set the drink on the bare wood tabletop.

The guy shakes his bronze-brown hair. "Nothing." He takes out a hundred dollar bill and hands it to me.

It's been so slow I wonder if Royal will even have the change in anything but fives and tens.

"You're new around here."

He stirs his drink. "I've been around and about these parts for a long time."

"New to Prancer's, then?"

"Yes."

"Well, enjoy!" We were trained as cocktail waiters to be friendly, but not to the point of bugging the patrons. If they start responding with one word answers, I take that as a cue to ring them up and bring back change.

But then the guy says, waving his hand, "Keep the change."

I stare at the hundred in my hand not quite believing what he's just said. Sometimes tips are big, but this is rare.

"You realize you gave me a hundred for a ten dollar drink."

"Yes."

I stare at him. His smile makes something inside my chest tug. Hard. Well, he is really handsome. And so far he hasn't been forward like some patrons who pant lasciviously or check me out with their gazes going up and down my body. In fact, he hasn't checked me out at all. It's kind of a turn-on. Make me work for it, I think. Make me beg.

"Thank you," I say aloud, and tuck the bill in the tip cup on my tray.

I return to the bar. The guys sitting there have already been waited on. I have no other customers, so I keep checking the cute daddy out the corner of my eye.

He's taking little sips through the two skinny red straws I'd put in the drink, but the level on the drink doesn't go down. I don't have an excuse to go back over until I see that maybe he needs a refill.

He's not checking out the bar. He's not looking hungry for a hook-up, but what do I know? Maybe he has a strategy I haven't noticed yet. He does check his phone once in a while, but that's about it.

Now he's got me wondering. Is he lonely? Was he just thirsty and so he stepped in? Is he even gay?

At the moment I ponder that last thought, he glances up. Straight toward me. Our gazes meet and he does not flinch.

Just then, Royal comes up to where I'm half-standing, half-sitting, having hitched my left buttock on the bar stool.

"Angelbaby, pay the till. Ten bucks for that drink." Royal gestures at my tray.

"Oh. Yeah!"

I grab ten bucks in change from my tip cup and walk around the bar to the register. I set my tray down and ring up the drink. The hundred I keep nice and folded inside the other bills, mostly fives, in my cup.

With that one tip, my night doesn't feel so much like wasted time now.

I grab my tray and go back out front. Waiting for more customers. Trying not to yawn.

8

I glance again at the velvet-clad daddy. I don't know why I'm calling him that nickname. He doesn't really look old. But he does look like someone who's been around the block, someone who is in charge. Maybe he runs a big company. Maybe he bosses guys around all day. Or maybe he is a loner but a control freak.

And there I go again speculating on him when I don't even know his name.

Just then, I see him wave at me, that beautiful smile of his crawling into my heart.

I walk over to him slowly; if he wants to check me out I've got no problem with that.

When I get to his booth, a little shiver runs down my spine. It's not fear or anything; it's more of a thrill. This guy has my attention, that's for sure. Usually, I leave work at work. I don't go home with too many from this bar. I'm no virgin, but I'm not into casual, either. I flirt for the job and then I clock out.

What am I waiting for? Like anyone, the perfect hero to sweep me off my feet. I know better. It's stupid. But I'm young. I've got time to play. And wait.

"Need a refill?" I ask. I blink a bit because I'd swear his hair just got a tad shinier and the tan on his cheeks has started to glow even more than when he came in from the cold. His eyes look like there are little blue lights shining from deep within.

His hand, which is resting on the side of his glass, is big but tapered and long, perfect, and a wide silver band decorates his middle left finger. It catches the light overhead, blinding me for a moment like someone far off holding a mirror to the sun and flashing it as a signal.

"Are you allowed to sit and talk while on duty?" the daddy asks.

I shrug. "It's a slow night." Royal won't care unless the place starts to get busy.

He gestures for me to sit, and in that moment I smell Christmas so strong in the air. Peppermint and pumpkin spice. Pine and sugar cookies.

"My name is Nic," he says.

"Nice to meet you, Nic."

"Is your name really Angelbaby? I heard your boss call you that."

"It's Angelo, actually, but outside of work everyone calls me Angel."

His lips curve up at that statement.

I lean one elbow on the edge of the table and drum my fingers on the smooth surface.

"So, how long have you lived in Alaska?" I ask.

Nic's eyes squint a bit. His smile goes flat, then up-curved again. "I don't actually live here. But I travel through often."

"So you're from the lower states? Or Canada?" I'm trying to place an accent, but his intonation is pretty flat.

"Hmm. I live pretty far north. Near the Canadian territory of Nunavut."

I'm not stupid, but I'm not up on my geography, either. The only area close to Nunavut, if my memory is serving me correctly, is the North Pole. But he can't mean that literally. It's just too funny. His hat, his boots, the red velvet. I called him Santa in my mind, but for fun, not because I believe it.

A chuckle escapes me before I can hold it back. I laugh when I'm nervous sometimes and I hate that about myself. I already look younger than twenty-two and I hate that I'm often seen as a silly teen, a kid who is immature. I'm well read and damn smart, but no one's ever going to find that out about me if I keep working jobs that require no shirt and I giggle after every sentence I utter.

But why am I nervous? This is simply a high-tipping customer. I have nothing to worry about, I tell myself. But wow, he's so handsome. Totally to my taste. Alluring, in fact. My flirting here in Prancer's is mainly a game, but it doesn't feel like that at the moment.

"It's pretty damn cold up there year round." My voice comes out rough. I clear my throat.

"It is." Nic nods. His eyebrows rise. "It's pretty cold here, too."

"Yeah, a holiday in Hawaii sounds good about now."

"I've been to Hawaii. But I prefer the cold," Nic says. "The snow. And the stars in the endless nights of the north."

I blink. "Yes, it is beautiful. So, you sound like a guy who can live anywhere he wants but you choose ice and snow."

He shrugs. "I have commitments in the northern territories."

"Ah. Yes. Work. A company man."

"In a manner of speaking." He does not elaborate, which only makes him more mysterious. And, to my lonely heart, enticing.

Most guys brag about their jobs, especially if they are wealthy. He strikes me as the wealthy sort, but so far not pompous about it. Definitely a charmer, this one, but not overt like he's coming onto me or anything. Which, of course, tallies even more points for me to favor him.

Again, the scent of Christmas wafts over me. I inhale with a sigh. It smells so good.

He has taken the two red straws I'd added to his drink and set them neatly on a Prancer's napkin. Now he sips his rum and Coke and it's halfway gone.

"Can I get you another?"

"In a moment." His gaze encompasses me and my skin goes warm. "Tell me about yourself, Angel. Like, for example, if you had a wish, what would it be?"

"A wish? You mean like world peace or something?"

"No. Not what you think is a right and proper wish. A selfish wish. Something for you and you alone."

It's weird to have a Santa daddy asking me this. I mean, seriously? Fuck, should I be sitting on his lap or something? My cheeks heat at the thought.

I suppress another chuckle; my lips press together until my front teeth dig into them.

"Anything?"

He nods.

"Like materialistic?"

Another nod. "Anything."

"Well, there are some very private ones." I lower my chin, playing a little coy. "But other than finding true love, I would say I wish for, um, well, I don't know. When I was a kid I asked for a green Schwinn bicycle with metallic handles. I never got it. It was too expensive. But I wanted it so bad. Is that the kind of wish you mean?"

So weird. Here I am telling him about a childhood wish as if he really *is* Santa.

"You would need an all terrain bike around here," he comments.

"Yeah." I shrug. "Mostly, I'm not the outdoorsy type. Not anymore. I go to the gym a couple times a week. That's it."

I rest my hand on my chin as I watch Nic drain the rest of his drink. I hop up, grabbing the empty glass. "Another?"

11

Nic shakes his head. "What I'd really like this time is a glass of milk."

"Uh, I don't think we have that. I can check." I don't say it aloud, but I'm thinking: *Milk and cookies would really go with your Santa coat.*

He waves his hand. "Not a problem." He stands. "I need to get going anyway."

I take two steps back, sorry to lose him so soon after we just met. I watch as he fastens his fur-lined red parka and puts on his fluffy Santa cap.

He's so tall and broad, just like I like 'em. And I like the creases in his face, like dimples that have deepened with time. I adore the gold-pink color of his cheeks, and the way his dark blue eyes dance in the lights of the bar. And his hair has a crinkly shine, both dark and light at the same time.

I always love the tall ones, brawny enough to hold me tight, or even lift me up if they are so inclined. Most are not so inclined. Most don't like to play the way I do. From the straightest to the gayest, they are more burly Alaskan types, the mountain men I fantasize about, yes, but their personalities are too straight-laced. And most are hunters, and more on the wild side. I don't like hunting, never did. It's a deal-breaker for me if someone isn't nice to animals.

Maybe I'm just not cut out for living in Alaska despite being born here.

I watch as Nic strides toward the front door. For a second, he stops as if he's about to turn back to me. But then his hand reaches for the inner door and opens it.

After he is outside, I walk to the front window to see him strolling into the steady sleet, sure-footed, shoulders back and head up as if he doesn't feel the ice and cold at all.

He goes to the street and starts down the walkway on foot. He has no car. Nothing. Which surprises me. I watch him, a flash of red under an occasional streetlight, until he is gone.

My demeanor slumps. Even though I don't date customers, I had liked the guy. Maybe a little too much too fast.

I go back to his table and start to clean it.

The napkin sits to the side and I pick it up. Then I see below the Prancer's logo is something handwritten. I start to read.

*Angel, I'd like to see you again some time. If you have such a wish, call this number.*

The number is smeared a little, but I can read it. I had had my eye on him this whole time and I never saw him write that note. Very strange. And the way he uses the word wish again.

I think I've already fallen in love.

# Chapter Two

*Nic*

The cold clings to this climate. The very air defines it. Ice shooting around me like little stars. Sludge at my feet, the frozen currents causing tiny tsunamis at the edges of my boots.

I feel none of it. Yet, I love it. The pattering of crystal shards, the wind trying to decide which way to turn, how the light catches the edges of ice and turns it into rainbows. Everything has a beautiful side if you look closely enough. But people, they are another matter. Some are nice. Some are not.

This is a hard world. This is a strange Earth. But with the exception of one night a year, mostly I stay away from humans. It is my personal choice. But sometimes a man, even one from an immortal race of elves, gets lonely.

The elves who work for me, and those who live in the hidden City of the North, are not of the same race as I. They are mortal, though very long-lived. They view me as their king.

I didn't ask for the job, but my magic created the hierarchy. I am their king, and I will not abuse that responsibility. So I live alone but for my servants. And though I have heard the rumors the elves spread about me once having had a wife, it isn't true. Even back on our dying native home world, before our escape through the portal to this Earth, I had lived alone. I had been younger then, and still thought I had all the time in the universe to find a lover among my people and make a family.

But here, in this realm, I am the only one of my kind. The only one who wields magic, which I always try to use for good.

I feel uneasy mixing personal with professional. Elves are my profession. I care for them, but I also rule them. I am their boss.

So when I get too lonely, I go into the human world for company.

It's rare. I've had three human lovers in two hundred years. Two of the relationships did not last past the second date. I never told them my secrets. But one I did confess my nature to after I felt our love had grown. He ran away and never contacted me again.

After that, I resigned myself to a fate of being alone.

So why did I walk into Prancer's tonight of all nights? Why did I even glance at the waiter who brought me my drink?

A loneliness I can no longer control rules me.

Angel. Angelbaby. I can't stop thinking about him. Sleek and young. Probably too young for me. But something about him quickened me, made my icicle blood flow and the ache in my chest swell.

Look at me. The first cute boy I meet on a lonely walk and an innocent dalliance in a gay bar and I'm already wanting. Leaving my number on a used napkin. Behaving like a dirty lonely old man in my thoughts.

But his skin was smooth like light, his body sleek where the lean muscles rippled. And his voice came over me like a low hum when he'd asked me for my order. Pretty boy with pretty hair and slim arms and a lean waist, the kind I like to wrap my large hands around.

This is getting me nowhere. I can't keep a human lover. I have proven this to myself. I don't need a lover anyway. My life is full of love. My elves love me. My reindeer are like my children.

I have a room full of fantasies behind a locked door, a room I rarely enter, but it's there just in case. My toys grow dusty in there, my adult toys, but I can dream and imagine quite well. I don't need the reality of this Earth where humans are struggling to find their way, and war and politics rule the day.

I'm fine in my own little world.

I tell myself this as I walk through a storm I don't feel, pressing myself into the beautiful shadows of darkness patched only by brave dim streetlights fighting to push back the night.

My vacation away from Santa's Village is something I do for myself every late November. For two weeks I leave the North Pole and rent a cabin with a fireplace and live away from the hectic elf mayhem that accompanies the approach of Christmas. Sure, I have my own castle, but every day there is full of messages and requests and my servants bustling about.

Every year, for two weeks, I take this time to be alone.

I had not planned on stepping one boot into Prancer's until I saw the lights of the establishment from the road.

I had not planned on meeting anyone, let alone a boy as compelling as Angel.

No, none of this had been on my agenda.

As I walk through the ripples of icy air, I decide if he does call I will ignore it. I will watch the call on my cell phone go to voicemail. I will never listen to the recording.

No one walks in the chill of an Alaskan night—or even day—in late November. No one is even out driving in this neck of the woods. I have the road to myself as I trek the two hour walk back to my cabin. I love to walk. I have energy to spare all the time, my magic flowing through me more and more every year.

The night encases me. I feel a part of it. I hadn't lied to Angel when I told him I'd been to Hawaii. I've been all over this strange and interesting world. I prefer the darker corners and shadows, not because I'm skulking, but because I am made of shadow more than light. My heart is full and loving and kind, but light is not where I am from. I am a strain of immortal elf from an ancient line.

Even back on our home world, we were rare, of a breed from a darker time, a shadow-breed of elf that subsisted more on the dark ions of winter than the light of summer. We love the stars and the fires that can only burn brighter on colder, darker nights. We are the intrinsic fairy essence of the yang side which beams under moonlight and the lace of cloud.

I've never lost that nature after centuries of life. I love my paradise of the north.

As I approach my cabin, scents of evergreen and peppermint fill the air. I've put a Christmas spell around the cabin, like a cloak of protection from that most popular book and movie series: *Harry Potter*.

The scent it gives off is from my essence, my Santa brand. My brand is associated with Christmas scents of this Earth, holiday meals and desserts, sweets, smoke curlicues from chimneys, pine and berry, gingerbread and sugar cookies. I was born with this essence and I will carry it with me into the Forever on the day I decide to fade into the immortal realms.

Inside the cabin, I've used my magic to transform it for the two weeks I'm here.

Holly and evergreen decorate the hearth and every shelf and bookcase. Electric candles weave in and out of the greenery. The cabin

16

came furnished but I refurbished, of course. The couch before the hearth is a large, plush red velvet—red is my favorite color. Christmas pillows are piled upon it—one shaped like a snowman.

A big screen TV hangs on one wall. The kitchen counter, which is an island dividing the kitchen and living room, is piled high with my favorite treats. My constitution is sugar-based, so most of the food is sweets and desserts. Pies, cakes, cookies, bowls of chocolate covered nuts and candy.

For humans, this much sugar is toxic. Too many rich foods cause them to gain weight, or even die. But I'm not human. My weight never fluctuates despite much of mythology and legend that depicts me as fat and round-cheeked.

In the bedroom, I have re-done the bed to be a king-sized mattress with full padding nestled in a frame shaped like a red sleigh. It's a bit much, but I love playing with my magic like its art, like sculpture. My creative mind is endless. Even my ice castle back in Santa's Village is piled high with too much decoration, but I love it. For me, it feels like safety. It's the nesting place of my fairy soul.

Tonight I'm tired.

In the bedroom, I set my phone by the nightstand, take off all my clothes and crawl beneath the red and green comforters. I don't need them for warmth, I simply like them. The cozy, secure feel of them surrounding me. The softest pillow cushions my head.

I fall into a dreamy sleep with visions of Angel dancing in my head.

\*

My phone wakes me.

Only my servant staff have this number. The elves in the stables and workshop must email me if they need something, or go through my servants.

I push myself up, the heavy covers falling away from my shoulders, and pick up my phone.

I don't recognize the number calling. I could let it go to voicemail, but instead, I swipe the answer button and say, "Hello."

"Is it too early? Did I wake you?"

The voice is unfamiliar. Young.

"Who is this?"

"Is this Nic? It's Angel. From last night?"

I rub my eyes, blinking away the last vestiges of sleep. Then my memory returns. I had gone into a gay bar called Prancer's, a gay bar with a cartoon logo of my beautiful reindeer jumping over the moon like some cow from a childhood Earth poem.

"Angel?" The beautiful boy who waited on me and sat down to tell me his wishes? Angelbaby, they called him. So sweet-faced. Body glowing with youth.

"Yeah. Uh. You left your number on your napkin. The little note was addressed to me. So. Here I am. Calling."

He sounds almost reticent, shy.

My body tingles in pleasure at his voice. "Yes. I'm glad you did."

"Your note said you might want to, um, get together? I think I'd like that. Uh, that is unless you've changed your mind." He starts talking faster. "Normally, I don't go out with patrons from Prancer's. It's work, you know? But, well, I, um--"

"I see. I am flattered, then."

Already, I am breaking my promise to myself to let this one go. There is something that pushes me for more with him—maybe the sound of his voice, or maybe the memory of his sweet body standing before me. I'm over three hundred years old. Normally not so shallow. But this boy's sweetness for the short time we talked lingers in my mind.

He makes a sound like a half-laugh. "I'm the one who's flattered. I mean, I get that a lot at work, but you were different. Something felt, um, just nicer."

Naughty. Nice. Either way works for me on this level.

I sit up, my back against more pillows, my knees bent. I'm naked in bed, talking to a pretty boy. This hasn't happened to me in far too long. He's of the generation on this world that is big on what they call hookups. I don't know if that's what Angel wants but I'm a little more formal despite my fantasies and my secret room back at my castle. I like to lead into my so-called hookups.

"Would you like to join me for dinner," I say.

"Yeah. Hell yeah. Just say when."

"When do you get time off from—from Prancer's?"

"Today's my day off."

"How about tonight, then?"

"Sure!"

I can hear he's trying not to sound too eager. My ego is definitely boosting on the romantic scale.

We set a time and he gives me his address.

Now I have to arrange for a car. My team is at my beck and call; the reindeer can be quickly readied, as well as my sleigh, at my mere magic whistle. But I don't think Angel is ready for that sort of transportation just yet.

When we hang up, I get up and shower and dress, excited to spend time planning for this date. I haven't felt this spring in my step since last Christmas Eve.

Angelo. Angel. Angelbaby. This lovely boy deserves the best.

# Chapter Three

*Angel*

He's picking me up at six.

What to wear?

Nic doesn't seem like the kind of guy who's going to take me to the roadhouse for a beer and a burger. I'm expecting more so fancier is better, I decide. And even if I do end up at a burger joint, at least I'll look better than everyone there.

My vanity is not something I'm ashamed of. It got me the job at Prancer's. It's getting me this date with a dreamy guy who could wrap me up almost double in his arms. Ah, how that red velvet shirt would feel against my skin!

I'm trimmed, my body hairs short, all over. I sleep practically fucking drenched in baby oil. It's all for the tips at work. Mostly. But more than clothes, I'm a tad vain about my sleek naked body, too.

Maybe I'll get to show it off.

I get out my streamlined black suit and a crisp, pink button up. A thin purple tie makes me look cool, not completely formal. I add several silver rings to my hands, and a couple jingle bracelets, silver and black.

My crazy dark blond curls are easily tamed back with enough mousse and hairspray, but I leave a couple dangling over my eyes. Yeah, I'm the kid who just flew in off the wind. Look at me, black winged with my hair in my face.

Does my look attract the more mature guys? I haven't had so much luck with that so far. If I were in Hawaii I'd be wearing red swim trunks all day, and go topless or wear a tight T-shirt with the word *Boy* printed across it in baby blue lettering. Whatever.

I'm in Alaska. My green parka is going to cover the suit anyway until we get to the restaurant. My knit cap will mess with my hair, too. It goes with the territory. But I think this Santa daddy isn't going to be shallow about all that. It's me who likes to look a certain way.

I'm ready a half an hour early. Eager much?

I hang out with other guys sometimes, but I don't really do the hook ups. I haven't done a real date in a long time.

It's nice sitting here waiting for Nic. Nice to think about how attractive he is, and how polite, not like the guys my age who leer and tell dirty jokes we have all heard a hundred times since we were sixteen.

I'm on my couch with the TV on, but I'm staring at the front door. In case Nic wants to come in, I've put everything in its place. My kitchen is spotless, which is the way I like it. When I was younger, I lived with roommates. I hated it. Such slobs.

Now I get to have everything my way.

I keep glancing out the window. The street is a thick, satiny black line with pools of gold dampness under the streetlights. Snow banks it in mini white cliffs. Cars drive by, their lights glittering, their tires making sizzling sounds on the asphalt.

A knot forms in my stomach just below my belly button. As the clock on my mantel approaches six, the tangle grows tighter. I guess I care about how this date goes. A lot.

Something about Nic resonates. Last night I even dreamed of him.

As I'm watching out my front window, a black Camaro pulls up to the curb by the pathway that leads to my front door. Nic gets out in his red cap and red fur-tipped parka and black boots.

My stomach flips over.

I turn off the TV and jump up, practically running to the door. I hear the clomp of boots on my walkway. I open the door, trying not to grin too wide.

The cold air hits my body with a sting. Every muscle tenses.

Nic smiles at me. "You look ready."

"Yes!" Behind the door, I grab my parka, scarf and cap. I hesitate. Should I invite him in? But he's more formal. It's too soon.

I jump over the threshold, donning my jacket, putting on my cap. Shit, my hair won't look right for the rest of the night, but oh well.

Nic reaches me, takes my scarf from my hand and arcs it over my head, wrapping it around me until it falls just right over my left shoulder. I am not sure why I find that gesture so hot.

"Hungry?" he asks.

"Very." I follow him to the car where, a complete gentleman, Nic opens the passenger door for me, then closes it as I settle in. The seat is warm on my ass, and I realize he thought of everything, even turning on the seat warmers so I'd be comfortable.

There's no rain or sleet tonight, but the air is like breathing crystal ice shards. My lungs ache. Tonight the temperatures are supposed to plummet even more than last night.

Welcome winter.

Nic gets into the driver's seat with a blast of cold air and turns on the engine. Warmth circulates about me. My cheeks heat up, burning.

"There's an Italian restaurant a few miles away," Nic says.

"I love Italian." I realize I'm still grinning.

"Excellent."

As he drives, his hands are lit from the dash lights. I admire the leanness of his long fingers curved around the steering wheel, and the veins on the backs of his hands.

If possible, tonight he's even more mesmerizing than when he walked into Prancer's. His scent is cider and pine. His face looks smooth and young in the shadows of the car, and his presence beside me makes me feel warm, safe and, damn it all, aroused.

I'm not ashamed of being aroused, don't get me wrong. Even if it feels a little naughty—and that also gives me a thrill, I'm not a teen anymore. I have some control if not my pride. I mean, working at a gay bar makes a person a little jaded, even if they are still young. I didn't think he would get under my skin so fast.

But he's so much my type.

I jokingly called him Daddy in my mind as I waited on him last night. But now? I wonder if he's okay with that scene for real. He's such the perfect guy for a daddy scene.

I squeeze my thighs tight as the mere thought makes my cock move under all my layers. I think: *This guy could really put me in my place.* Which of course doesn't help matters down below at all.

To distract myself, I start the small talk. "What is it you do for a living?"

"Hmm. It's complicated. I run a toy manufacturing company. And, well, sort of a delivery service."

His rich voice makes my skin tingle. I barely hear him.

"That's cool." That means he's rich, which doesn't really figure into my like or dislike of him, since I make my own way in the world just fine, thank you. But it does lend him an air of even more respectability and mystique. Last night he mentioned he travels a lot, and that paints him in an experienced light.

I like experienced men, educated men, men who are in charge.

I take a deep breath and it hisses a little through my teeth.

"Warm enough?" Nic asks.

"Fine." I smile into the darkness.

When the car pulls up to the restaurant, an array of colorful, festive lights greets us. Some of them line the fence of the walkway leading up to the restaurant's porch. Others outline the A-framed building. Three outdoor light trees grace the yard by the pathway.

Everything is crisp and clear and bright. I love Christmas lights. I blink several times, like I'm in a dream.

"I can already smell the food."

Nic walks close beside me. "You will order whatever you like. Tonight's on me."

"Thank you." I smile up at him.

No guy my age would be so graceful. And a bit formal. I love it.

When we reach the foyer, warm air rushes around me again. Nic starts to take off his jacket. Quickly, the male host wearing a white shirt takes it from him, along with his cap and scarf, and hangs it on a long line of hooks by the door.

Before I can make a move, Nic turns and helps me off with my own parka and the scarf he'd wound me up in. I feel quite taken care of. I've worked hard to be on my own, but this feels good. In my private life, having someone care for me in this way is heady.

The host hangs everything up, then immediately directs us to a table draped in a white cloth edged in lace. A square cut crystal container holds an orange, dancing flame, making the silverware laid out on cotton white napkins glitter just below the shining bread plates.

A waiter hurries over with warm bread and butter for us, and fills our glasses from a water-beaded silver pitcher.

The host pulls out the chairs and helps us get them in place. Everything is fine and perfect and rich. I would have been just as happy at a steakhouse, but this is elegant for a first date, and I love it.

The waiter hands each of us a menu, and then bows.

I look over the offerings. I know what I love, so it's not a difficult decision. Decadence is the word to describe this place so far, so I'll indulge. Chicken alfredo. If I were counting calories tonight, it would be devastating. Instead, my mouth waters.

The waiter returns with a wine menu.

Nic looks at me. "Yes?"

I nod. "You pick."

"White or red?"

I always go for white. But this time I shrug.

Nic raised one dark eyebrow, then turns to the waiter. He points to a brand.

The waiter nods and asks, "The chardonnay or the sauvignon blanc?"

"Sauvignon blanc."

Exactly what I would have chosen. I don't say anything, but I lower my head and look at Nic through my eyelashes in approval.

The wine comes and we give our order. It turns out Nic orders exactly the same dish I do but sans the chicken. He actually orders veggie alfredo.

We're *almost* a match!

I try not to laugh at myself.

When the waiter leaves, Nic tells me he doesn't eat meat, but makes no big deal out of it. He says with a sparkly smile, "When you're out with me, you eat anything you wish."

We talk over dinner about what I call know-nothings. But it's necessary when getting to know someone. Turns out, Nic is a bit short on words when it comes to talking about himself. He keeps bringing me out of myself, making me elaborate until I feel I'm monopolizing the entire conversation.

I tell him about my childhood where both my parents worked but it was still hard. I had to take care of myself a lot of the time from age eight on. I didn't mind. I was resourceful and smart even that young.

He wants to hear more. All the details of my household, my parents, the fact that I'm an only child.

"You sound like you grew up fast," Nic says.

I nod. "A little. But lack of supervision meant I also got into trouble."

"Oh?"

24

"Sure. You know kids. I hung with an older crowd. I was ten when I tried my first cigarette, and came home coughing up a lung. My dad could smell it on me. My parents are very anti-smoking, anti-drug. Super straight laced. My dad was so mad. I thought he was going to hit me. I was grounded for two weeks."

Nic laughs, his eyes narrowing.

"I don't smoke anymore just in case you're wondering. It was a lark."

Nic shrugs.

"I did the usual," I continued. "I got caught shoplifting. Of course the gang I hung out with always used me as the scapegoat because I was littlest, and the cutest. Sometimes I could whip up the tears and cry my way out of a scene. After I got us out of trouble that way a few times, the guys would treat me better. But most of the time they ignored me. I just wanted to belong somewhere, that's all."

"That's what anyone wants," Nic says.

"Yeah." I let my gaze fall away to stare at my plate of half-eaten alfredo. The portion size had been huge. Nic had eaten all of his.

"I went through a period of acting out, though. Once, my dad was so frustrated with me, he actually put coal in my stocking that year."

"You know Santa never really leaves coal in stockings," Nic says. As if he knows this firsthand. "At least, not in modern times. In the past, coal was essential for many families in various parts of the world to keep warm during winter. It could be very expensive, so it could have been considered a real gift."

I lean against the edge of the table. "I never thought of that. I was always taught bad boys and girls get coal."

"Huh. More like a rod or a birch switch would be my idea." Nic winks at me.

Was that a come on? Seriously, the idea of a switch has me both squirming in my seat and hot at the same time. But looking at Nic, I decide he's probably never taken a switch to anyone in his life.

"There are traditions that go back hundreds of years," Nic says. "Before the Santa tradition, there is the myth of some sort of traveling person leaving coal for bad children as winter gifts. But Santa, well, he never did in any of the myths, except in a few fictional poems and songs."

"But it's *all* fiction," I say.

"Is it?" Another wink.

I laugh. This guy has me hook, line and sinker. Is it too early yet to say I think I love him?

Dessert comes but I'm already full. Tiramisu. Nic eats his in about three bites. I pick at mine. I already have a box wrapped with my leftovers ready to take home.

Home. Is that where this date will end? With Nic taking me back home and me spending the night alone? I wonder. First dates traditionally call for no fraternization. But those aren't fast and hard rules. Not for me, anyway.

But for Nic?

So many questions! He has listened to me ramble on for so long, but has still told me so little about himself.

"So, where's your place?" I blurt.

"I have several. But here I have a cabin out by Summerwood."

"Oh, it's pretty over there."

"It's pretty throughout this state."

"True." I tap my fork against the sugary concoction on my plate.

"Would you like to see it?"

"What?"

"My cabin." Nic takes a sip of the glass of milk he ordered with dessert. I don't know too many guys who drink milk. It's a little funny, but for Nic to do it is so endearing. My heart revs up.

"I'd adore seeing your cabin," I reply. It's a fast move on a first date. But the world doesn't end at my statement. Nothing blows up. The waiter simply brings the bill in a shiny leather folder.

Nic seems in no hurry, though. He sits back and watches me through half-closed eyes. I don't know if it's hunger I see there, or simple curiosity. Or both. Both would be nice. Nicer if we were alone and in his cabin. I can't wait to see it.

The waiter checks on us to see if we want more of anything. I shake my head no.

Nic says, "We're fine."

I am basking in an afterglow of rich food and a handsome date. I'm super fine. Like I just had great sex, only not. I laugh at myself, this time out loud.

"You're happy," Nic observes.

"Yes."

26

"Good. When is your next day off?"

"Why are you asking?" I crumple my napkin from my lap and put it on the table for something to occupy my restless hands.

"Because I'd like to have another date with you."

"Well, this one isn't finished yet."

"No. But I like to plan things." He takes a deep breath and graces me with a big smile.

"Yeah. Well, I work a lot. Always nights." I try not to show my disappointment in my own words. "Five days a week. My next night off isn't until Tuesday." That's two days away. I usually get Sundays. And Prancer's is always closed on Tuesdays.

"Will you keep Tuesday open, then?" Nic asks.

"Yes." My voice comes out soft and rippling from my throat. This dynamic suits me. I like being wined and dined. I like that my date already wants a second date with me, when neither of us knows yet how this one will end.

Finally, Nic pays the bill and we rise to leave.

The night has grown colder as we step outside. The Christmas lights flash in my eyes. Everything smells of fresh pine, wintergreen mint from the candy I grabbed from a tray on the way out, and still that sugary cookie scent, which I am convinced is some sort of aftershave Nic wears.

The chilled air steals breath from my lungs, but the valet already has our car waiting, running and warmed up inside. He blows into his gloved hands, then holds them out as Nic tips him a bill I cannot see the denomination of. But I already know he's a great tipper.

Nic drives off down the wet, dark road and into a part of town I don't see often since it's more into the wilderness territory. I am neither a camper, hunter nor hiker.

"So where are we going?" I ask again, just to be sure.

"Summerwood. You did say you wanted to see where I live."

"But sir," I fake-protest. "I hardly know you."

"I promise I will take you home at any time you ask me to."

"Fair enough." I grin again, hoping the shadows hide my youthful eagerness.

The drive is not long. But it's definitely in the middle of nowhere, perhaps five or six miles from town. Nic pulls the Camaro down a darker, heavily wooded, single lane road, and slows. The pavement ends and the car bumps along snowy slushy dirt for a very short way before I see his driveway and the cabin.

It can't be easy for him to get in and out of here if he's snowed in, but then maybe the plows make it this far. Or he shovels. He has big enough biceps showing through his clothes to do the job in a few hours.

Tonight his dark blue suit showed ample muscle at dinner. It had been difficult to look away from the vision of him. Crisp white shirt. A bright red handkerchief in his pocket decorated with a sprig of embroidered holly.

Neither of us had informed the other of what the date might be like. We'd both shown up in suits. I liked how we already thought the same. Ha ha, I like to think somewhere in the cosmos two stars are already lining up.

Nic pulls into a garage next to the cabin. The door automatically opens for him as if sensing something in the car. He doesn't push a remote or anything.

Once the car is stopped, but before I can open the door and get myself out, Nic comes around and opens my door.

Wow, now that is five star treatment.

We enter through his kitchen, which is clean but cluttered. The main countertop is piled high with saran-wrapped plates of cookies, pies, cakes. This guy has a major sweet tooth. Or maybe baking is his hobby when he's not working at his toy manufacturing company.

Through the space over the counter is the living room. My jaw drops.

Every surface is covered in glittery Christmas lights, festive greenery, and candles in glass holders. The hearth is dark, but logs are set inside for a perfect fire.

A Christmas tree stands in the corner by two windows, one looking east, one with a north view. It's lit up like a glittering sea in full moonlight. Shining ornaments spin and catch the light from every angle, spraying rainbow hues all over the room.

"Wow. This is amazing. You love Christmas, I guess. I don't even have a tree!"

"Well, you can enjoy mine while you're here." Nic turns. "Would you like some hot cider?"

"Yes!"

"I'll light the fire and we can sit on the couch, drink and enjoy the view."

I love the room, it's true, but I want to be enjoying the view of him even more.

I take off my hat and scarf and Nic helps me out of my parka. He hangs everything, including his own garments, on hooks by the door to the garage.

I move into the living room. Everything is warm and cozy-feeling. The couch seems almost alive. As I sit, it wraps me in cushiony comfort.

Nic comes in with the cider and hands me my mug. Steam rises from the liquid. I sniff and it smells wonderful.

Nic sets his mug down and quickly makes a fire. The light in the room brightens, wavering from the crackling and licks of the flames.

When Nic sits beside me on the couch, our legs brush. The suit trousers almost match, black to dark blue, the material thin enough I can feel his warmth against me. My blood flowing through my limbs seems as hot as the cider.

I know I want him. If he were an ordinary hook up, which I rarely do, I'd be making crude comments already, or snuggling up to him, forcing the issue. But with Nic that behavior does not naturally overtake me.

I'm not that shy, and rarely awkward, but this guy is different. I may have started out flirting with him at the bar because of his tip and his looks, but the more I get to know him and be with him, the more I like him in other ways, on multiple levels.

My left knee bobs up and down.

"You're not cold, are you?" Nic asks. Always caring, looking out for my comfort. He doesn't downright stare, but he notices me. Me. Like I'm the only star in the sky right now.

"No, it's fine. I'm so happy. I love your cabin and your style."

"My style," he begins. "Is not like others."

"I figured that out."

Suddenly, Nic gets a faraway look in his eyes. It makes me a little uncomfortable because he's always been present and in control.

"Tell me more about you," I say.

"What do you want to know?"

"Everything." I laugh.

His eyebrows rise. "Everything will take a long time to tell."

"Then I'll never get bored."

Nic smiles. "You're very sweet."

Okay, now here it comes. The brush off but in a polite way as if maybe he can pull it off so I won't notice. My spirits dive and my stomach goes heavy.

But then I remember. Nic has already made a date with me for Tuesday. My next day off. He can't get out of that easily. Not now.

"I'm not that sweet," I counter.

"Really?"

I nod, smirking.

He blinks, but then I think he's actually winking at me. "I would like to kiss you." Blunt and to the point, but still his words are gentlemanly, well mannered. I'm literally squirming on this couch now.

"I'd like that."

Our eyes meet. Since he's the one who asked, I wait for his first move. He lifts his hand and places the tips of his fingers along my cheek. Slowly, he moves it to the back of my neck and leans in. My mouth opens as if I have no volition left.

His lips touch mine with a hint of the cider he's just sipped. And something else. Something starry and clear and crisp, a sort of wind like we're flying but we're quite still and the room is warm from the fire and the glittering lights.

His kiss is velvet. His touch dry and firm until his tongue lightly touches my bottom lip.

Colors explode inside my mind at the contact. My mouth opens further as if to breathe him into me. The sensation of him this close sends rivers and currents of pleasure all through my limbs and down my spine to rest at the small of my back. My cock begins to fill.

Somewhere inside me a door opens. And there is a land I've never seen before, magnificent with snow like frosting on little cabins and the moon smiling down on snow-sugared avenues and lanes stretching toward glacier white cliffs. The stars are so plentiful they nearly blot out the blackness of the void.

I hear singing, distant, high and echoing, like the sweetest song floating on drifts of ice. The siren song fills me up near to bursting with nostalgia for something I've always wanted but never received.

30

Warmth and belonging. No longer alone for so many hours and days as I was when I was a kid.

I have never wanted to cry from a mere kiss.

My arms reach around Nic to embrace him because I want to be closer. I want more.

Nic embraces me in return, his one hand on the back of my neck to hold me to him, the other wrapping around my shoulders.

I make a groaning noise. I hear a drum like a heartbeat. My own guards fall away, my vulnerability now raw and exposed.

I gasp aloud and pull back.

Nic holds me, but does not force a return to the kiss. Instead, he watches me and I feel the need to explain.

"What is—I never—you're quite overwhelming."

"Does that mean you liked it?"

"Uh huh." I have no words to explain to him the magic of that kiss. I blink away the sweet sting in my eyes.

"Are you all right?" A whisper.

"It's not like I've never been kissed, but yet it was as if no one ever had until now." I smile to brush away the awkwardness of my words. "I'm just being childish."

"We're all children. We're just older children once we reach adulthood."

"True." I love how he speaks, the words he chooses. The way he is as if he cares so much when we have only just started this— whatever it is. Connection? Relationship? I have no idea.

"Perhaps you deserve more than you've been getting from others in matters of the heart," Nic says.

"I do?"

"Angel. Angelbaby. You live in a world of youth and exuberance and you should be enjoying it, of course. Your job, your ability to mesmerize others with your personality and your looks at the bar, is wonderful. But when I saw you, I sensed something else."

"What?"

"Something maybe you are missing? I don't presume to know for sure, but I know myself. I'm happy doing what I do, too, but fulfillment often eludes me. In other words--" His voice trails off.

"What?"

"I—I get lonely."

He speaks the words from my core, as if he's eavesdropped on my most private fantasies. "Yes." I nod. I blink away the eye-sting again. "Yes."

I'd wanted his hands on me, and more. I'd hoped for fantastic sex and walking a bit wobbly the next day with a grin on my face. But now with Nic that isn't enough. If I go all the way with him, I'm going to be hooked. I already acknowledged that the moment I saw him walk up my condo path to my front door.

"Please," I begin.

"Sweet Angelbaby, I know what you wish for. Other than that green Christmas bike." He laughs.

"Please." I nod more vigorously. "Kiss me again."

He pulls me to him and his mouth gently takes mine again in gentle strength and bursts of magic visions. Images of ghost-mist paths and white flowers and snowmen bending to touch the ground with their carrot noses. The tundra filled with rainbow lights. Golden windows promising home and hearth, warmth and love. Safety. Security.

I have always taken care of myself. I'm good at it. But now I let go as if I have fallen into his arms and into this kiss like I've been waiting a thousand years.

Nic is strong and generous at the same time. Holding and taking, giving and bestowing. My heart cannot keep up with my excitement. I want to burst everywhere, not just from my cock. I want to hang onto him and never let go.

It's ridiculous, of course. I have a life; he has a life. I have work tomorrow. He has his company to run.

But now feels like all there is. I'm floating in a white cloud of euphoria and we've barely touched.

The kissing is everything. All I ever want in the moment. The now. I want to rush. I want to hold still. I cannot make up my mind.

We stay like that, connected, until our cider grows cold and the fire drifts from its rapid wild peak to a slower flame.

Finally, Nic pulls away. I'm so happy I am floating in my mind and the room is a blur.

"Come along." His voice sounds far away. "We have Tuesday. Do not forget. But now you need to go home and get a good night's sleep."

I don't want to leave yet. The hour is—is, well, I have no idea what time it is. Early still. It must be.

"Not yet," I mumble, but on instinct I reach for my phone and turn it on. The time reads: 10:23 pm.

He came by my house at six sharp. Dinner lasted a couple hours at most. All we did was kiss. For an hour, it seems. An hour. And I'm in an altered state, the rush of Nic's touch going through me and melting every tense feeling I've ever stored within since childhood.

Suddenly I really do feel tired. I want Nic's arms around me again. I want to rest my head on his chest. But he stands and pulls me up by my wrist. He puts his hand on the center of my back.

"I will see you safely home, Angelbaby. And I will be seeing you again if you agree."

"I agree. But Tuesday seems so far off. I don't know if I can wait."

Nic laughs. "You will be fine. Come. Let's go now. We don't want to rush such a good thing when we have time. We have time."

Whatever he means by that, it comforts me. But I don't want to face the night out there, and the cold, not even for a simple drive home.

I push my lower lip out.

"No pouting." He laughs again. "Even if I might find it cute. But it's one of my rules."

"Rules, eh?"

Nic says, "Yes. I have rules. But don't worry. They are not hard to follow."

"I can't wait to learn them all," I say.

Nic grabs my parka, scarf and hat. He dresses me as if I'm a baby and I like it. He grabs his own coat but does not zip it. I've already seen that the cold does not affect him.

In the garage, he is the gentleman as always and opens the car door for me. I climb inside and wrap my arms around myself.

When we pull up to my condo, Nic leans in and kisses me again. Quicker this time, but still magical. Warm and infused with a pleasure I cannot describe.

How long have I been waiting for this man?

As I go to sleep alone in my own bed that night, I ponder this question deep into my dreams.

# Chapter Four

*Nic*

I lie awake into the night thinking of that kiss. Angel in my arms. This human boy who has angled his way into my heart. It's not an impossible scenario. But it is complicated.

I showed him my true self tonight. Just a slice of it, really, in that kiss. He pretty much collapsed in my embrace.

This is new for me. I have had few lovers in my life, and only three of them human. None of them ever saw my true self, and the one I began to tell my story to immediately ran away. I am not sure Angel can withstand elfin magic and fairy lore from another world that existed next door to his own.

My magic is powerful, but I do not use it to control others.

A wind curls its way around my cabin like a creature trying to get closer to my presence. I'm not like anyone on this Earth. Even the wind can feel it.

I don't feel old, though. Not by a long-shot. My life is full, but the loneliness of being the only one of my kind pervades. My moods remain jolly, but the elves have their lives, and I have mine. On darker days, I dream endlessly of someone to share it with.

There will come a day when I will fade, like all immortals including my flying reindeer. I will circumvent capture from the archive of the universe which records all that ever was and ever will be, and I will take on new forms and never die.

Most beings cannot accomplish this, but immortals weave beyond the fabrics of spacetime. I was taught by my grandmother. She was the wisest person I have ever known. We are from an ancient and rare race.

She used to tell me to look up at night at the stars. "Those are the eyes of your kin staring back at you."

It is a crushing realization, both sad and terrifying, overwhelming and wondrous. But the loneliness expands with every decade. No longer do I know anyone like me. Through the portal that led from our realm to this Earth, I am the only santa-elf who escaped along with my reindeer and a few hundred mortal elves.

I lie awake and think of Angel. I tell myself he's a lark, a distraction. Certainly he must be. Young, cute, human. It can't be serious. I'm so much older. I'm not human. And he is--well, he is a cocktail waiter at a gay bar. How does that make a match?

I shake that thought away. It sounds far too judgmental for my mood. He is a person. A true and real being of this Earth. So what if he is young and beautiful and flirty? I should be perfectly free to think of him beyond those more shallow attributes. I should be able to date him formally if I wish.

But also, what if I wish to focus on his nature? What if my body craves a contact with this boy that is not so formal and proper, but that is lovely and beautiful and artistic in its own way?

I need to stop dodging the issue. I crave sex as any other male of any species might.

I want Angel. That is the heart of it. My truth.

My body shivers and aches like the grieving wind searching for what it cannot seem to find.

When I admit to myself what I really wish for—a question I ask others but never myself—I realize I can have Angel and not need to worry about my secret self, my village at the North Pole, and letting slip the revelation that I have magical power.

He does not need to know these things for us to connect at first.

And if I want to keep him?

My heart hammers in my chest. The grief of wanting what I cannot have tries to rattle my fortitude. I tell myself I will cross that bridge when I come to it.

As I fall to sleep, dreams form around me. In one, Angel is encased in ice, the perfect form of an enticing young man. He waits for me, frozen, like a toy I've given myself to play with when I choose, when I want.

In yet another dream, Angel is chained to the crystal white wall of my ice castle in a hidden, secret room. I hold him there by my will and do whatever I want to him.

I wake with the images fading, disturbing me. Yet my inner self will not be denied. My fantasies belie reality; I would never bring harm to another against their will. But in my secret thoughts boys— young men--become my toys and I like it. And since coming to Earth,

35

my fantasies involve humans, never other elves. Exclusively male. I've never denied I am gay.

But there must be a name for that elf to human orientation—everything has a label these days—but I don't know what it is.

I wake the next morning restless and hot. I take a long shower and for breakfast eat a lot of sweets.

I have nothing to do. This is my vacation, so I relax and plan for tomorrow's date. It takes every bit of energy I have to not go to Prancer's and watch Angel work. It would be an intrusion. But it's difficult to resist.

I send Angel a text later in the afternoon.

*For our Tuesday date: less formal this time. Jeans will be fine.*

He texts me back right away.

*I'll wear my tightest ones.*

For a moment I cannot breathe. Tight jeans on that lithe body will be my undoing. How should I respond? Why am I, Santa of myth legend, tongue-tied around this boy?

I find myself mentally checking my lists—so many lists in my head. Boys and girls. Even adults. I mark a large P in front of them. Until I get to Angel's name. I press the stamp on the column to the right of him. C.

*P for present. C for coal.* I laugh.

In reality it's a code. I wouldn't give anyone coal and never have. But Angel might be my first.

I don't know what else to do, so I send him an LOL. My best effort is those mere three letters right now.

Tomorrow cannot come soon enough.

# Chapter Five

## Angel

The hours at work on Monday crawl by at such a slow pace, I think I am in a time loop. The weather is freezing, but there's no sleet or snow, so it is a little busier than when Nic came in on Saturday.

Guys flirt with me, but I don't see them. All I see is Nic's face. And his LOL text after I told him I'd be wearing tight jeans. I still feel his lips on mine. Every time I remember our long kiss, my mouth and body tingle.

I sling drinks. I clean up. My eyes focus on none of it.

"Angelbaby! Pay attention!"

Royal's voice stabs me just as a tray sitting too close to the edge of the counter tips. I try to catch the drinks but everything plummets to the floor with a splatter-crash.

Applause breaks out throughout the bar. I grin and take a bow.

I glance at Royal, who crosses his arms over his chest and squints at me. He doesn't have to say another word to convey his displeasure. I give a heavy sigh, grab some rags and a broom, and start to sweep up.

After that, despite my inattention to the job, I get good tips and a few phone numbers on napkins as well. All but the tips go into the trash.

After my shift is over at two in the morning, Royal takes me aside.

"Everything all right with you?"

"Sure. Why wouldn't it be?" I ask.

"I don't know. You tell me."

"Tired, I guess."

"Partying too hard? That's not my problem and not what I pay you for."

I start to roll my eyes, which he hates, but stop myself when he grabs my tip jar and spills it onto the counter. He begins to count it out. It's quite a lot for a winter Monday evening.

"They like you. But remember, no favors for big tips."

My face heats. I am used to all sorts of teasing from my customers. But not from Royal, insinuating I might do more sexual favors. He's my boss. I hate how his statement makes me feel.

"Favors? Like what?" I widen my eyes in innocence.

"You know what."

I don't do that sort of thing at Prancer's. Never on the job. Never off the job. But what can I say to make him believe me when I'm dressed in tight leather pants, no shirt and a sparkly red bow tie? I even wore a bit of glitter on my pecs today.

I may not be innocent, but I'm not guilty, either.

I stare at the money in Royal's hand, afraid maybe he'll dock my pay for the glassware I broke.

Silently, his gaze burning into me, he hands it to me. A stack of mostly fives and twenties and a couple hundreds.

"Yes, sir," I say, taking the money and folding it. "No favors. I hear you loud and clear." I make good money here. I need to keep this job.

In the back room behind the kitchen is a line of lockers. I go to mine and change into sweats and a sweater. I carefully hang my gaudy bowtie on the hook inside, and fold my leather pants. I have two pairs. I alternate. Usually one is at the cleaners. I certainly can't throw leather into my washing machine.

When I leave the bar the late night air makes me feel I'm being encased in ice despite my thick parka. I head to my BMW and quickly get in, hitting the button to turn on the seat warmers and starting it to get the hot air flowing. The fan comes on and the air comes out first as a freezing breeze.

I wait for my car to heat up, then pull out onto the highway.

I head east toward town. But when I get there, I don't take the turn to my complex. Instead, I keep going.

It's stupid, really. But I want to drive by Nic's place. Just because. Suddenly I feel like a total stalker. At the same time, a thrill ripples through me.

When I reach his turn off, the road narrows. His driveway is hard to find, but I can now see his cabin. I slow. All the lights outline every feature of the design of his abode. Like his home is made of Christmas glow and shadows and square gold windows.

My body starts to feel light, made of air. A tingle begins in my stomach and runs up and down my spine. Being this close to him, and I'm a goner.

My car tires grumble at the state of the asphalt. It's crumbly on the sides, and the road narrows even more.

I want to park and stare. I want to think of him inside eating his sweets and sitting by the fire. I hope he's thinking of me in return. I want to be near him again. I want to kiss him.

As my engine revs in the cold night air, I see another light appear, a rectangle of white. His front door has just opened. Out comes Nic, his tall frame silhouetted by the indoor light. He holds a large red sack, which is both funny and odd because, well, Santa Claus has a large red sack and he's always been *Santa* in my mind.

He moves down the porch steps and I watch him open the sack. I would swear I see stars coming from it. He shakes it over the ground. Flakes of light fall around him, lighting up his hair. He has on no jacket, no scarf. He's wearing a simple button up shirt. It's too dark to make out the color—maybe black, maybe red.

He shakes the sack one more time, then crumples it in one hand and stands glancing from right to left.

Slowly, they come out of the woods. First the buck with a full antler rack. Then a few does. Then two more bucks. They walk right up to Nic, bend their heads and begin to eat.

Now I get it. It was grain or corn he was spreading. Deer food. Used usually by hunters, but sometimes by those who just want to feed the wild beasts.

As the deer feed, they show no fear of Nic. He walks right up to the first buck and runs his hand down his tawny side, then up his neck to pet him behind the ears.

It's an amazing sight. The other deer pause from their feeding and move toward Nic, heads out. Nic pets each one in turn. I imagine he's telling them how beautiful they are, and that he means them no harm. I imagine he's telling them secrets he might never tell another human soul, not even me.

My car is still slowly moving. I need to turn around but my lights will hit the snow bank. Then Nic will see me. But he doesn't know what I drive. I never pointed out my car to him.

I move down the road and find a wide spot on the almost nonexistent shoulder to turn around. I curse when my wheels spin in the wet earth and slush. This ridiculous. I'm spying on Nic and now I'm going to get stuck.

I already made a fool of myself with Royal at work, and now here I am being more of one.

"Nic. I'm just so fucked up over you," I say to myself.

I start to move a little, holding my breath, but then my tires spin again with a loud hum of my engine.

"Fuck!" I bang on the top of the steering wheel. I'm facing out of the narrow road toward the highway, but I can't go anywhere.

Nic's bright home looms in my vision. I see Nic glance out over his property to the street. All is in silhouette, Nic, the deer surrounding him, the glimmering holiday lights as a backdrop. It's like some breathtaking Christmas card.

I blink and rev my engine again, trying to get out of there. But Nic already has seen me. He's moving down his driveway and through the snow in my direction.

Great. Fine. Just what I need. And now this wonderful guy is going to think I've creepily stalked him and never want to see me again.

I try once more to get off the shoulder but the tires kick up muddy sludge. I watch as Nic rounds the edge of his driveway and steps onto the road.

With a heavy sigh, I roll down the window.

He walks up, looking all big and strong, and says, "Hey, need a push?"

I lean my head out the window. "Uh, hi, Nick."

"Angel!"

"Would you believe me if I said I was just driving by?"

"At two-fifteen in the morning?" But he has a smile on his face as he says that.

"Yeah. I just got off work. I was driving around looking at Christmas lights?" I grimace as I realize I end the sentence in an up-tone like a question.

"I see." He narrows his eyebrows.

"We never had lights when I was a kid. My parents both worked and we didn't have time for them." Always go for the sympathy vote.

He does not accuse me of lying. Or spying. He says, "Would you like to come in for a warm drink?"

40

"It's so late. What are you doing up?"

"Me? I have always been a night-owl."

I glance at the front of his cabin. "Feeding the deer, I see."

He nods as he says, "Actually, I'm feeding my friends. This herd lives nearby."

"Yeah. Okay."

"Yes to having deer as friends? Or to that warm beverage?"

"Um. Uh, both?"

"Good answer. Come on. I'll give you a push and then you can go up the drive and pull in front of the garage."

My nerves nearly derail my excitement at seeing Nic again. It's been only a day and I missed him. I don't know what that means, but it's nice. And weird. But nice, mostly.

Nic heaves against my car and I push down on the gas pedal lightly. I don't want him covered in slushy goo. I barely hit the gas and it's as if my car lifts up and practically flies back onto the asphalt.

Nic jogs around to the front of my car and waves me forward. My headlights hit him. I now notice it is a red shirt he's wearing. He fills it out nicely.

Slowly, I follow him to his driveway and turn toward his cabin.

When I'm parked, he opens the car door for me. My gentleman. I follow him past the deer, who ignore us and continue to graze on the corn and grain he's thrown into the snow. We go up the light-strung porch and into his festive cabin.

"Go ahead and make yourself comfortable. I have tea, coffee, cocoa."

"Ohhh, something sweet for sure"

"Cocoa it is. I make it with milk so it's quite good."

My stomach growls. On nights I work late, I don't get much to eat. My lunch break, which occurs around nine at night, is twenty minutes and barely gives me time to scarf down a few beer-battered hot wings.

When Nic brings me a mug, I flash back on last night. Our date and the incredible kissing we shared on this couch.

Nic sits right beside me so we're actually touching. "So, what were you really doing skulking around my place?"

My skin grows hot. "I uh—I uh--"

He laughs. "It's all right if you don't want to say."

I close my eyes and inhale the chocolaty scent of my drink. It's obvious, isn't it? I'm totally infatuated with this man. I look up.

"So does this count as a second date, or is that not until tomorrow?"

"Hmm. Maybe both?"

"What does that mean?"

Nic shrugs. His eyes flicker. "If you stay through tomorrow and we go out at dinner as we planned, isn't that all one date?"

I blink hard. "Are you asking me to spend the night?"

"It's cold out and too late for you to drive all the way home, don't you think?"

I live about ten minutes away, but I don't argue it. I haven't stopped thinking about wanting Nic since I left last night.

"You are. Asking me. To spend the night."

Nic has a twinkle in his eye, but his smile drops away. He glances at the fire dancing in his hearth. "All right. I admit. I am."

"Then I say yes."

He turns with a big grin. "That's what I'd hoped to hear."

"Do we get to share a bed?" My boldness is one of my best features, I think.

Nic swallows hard. He picks up his mug and sips his cocoa. It's as if he has suddenly lost the ability to speak.

"Because I would like that," I quickly add.

"I would, too," he whispers.

I am good at sensing people and their moods. With Nic I get the impression he's not been with anyone in a while. Maybe a long while.

The cocoa is great, but I want to kiss Nic again. I can't stop thinking about kissing him.

I put my cocoa down and lean into him. "I should not have done what I did, barging in on you, but I'm not sorry I'm here now."

"Are you tired after work?"

"No. After work I'm always hyped up."

Nic sets his cocoa on the coffee table next to mine and turns on the couch with one knee bent, facing me. "I am glad you're here, too."

I tilt my head. "Were you thinking about me?"

"In fact, I was." He holds my gaze.

I grin. "I couldn't stop thinking about you all night at work."

"Did you let anyone touch you tonight?"

42

A little surprised at his question, I shake my head. "Why? Are you jealous of my job?"

"I don't know. I don't think I'm the jealous type. But you work topless, and you flirt, don't you?"

"Sure. It gets me tips."

"Is that what you did with me?"

I shake my head, wondering where this is leading. "Honestly, no. You caught my attention the moment you walked in. Something—I don't know. You're amazing. I felt drawn to you."

Nic smiles.

"Just so you know, I don't let the customers touch me for tips. Okay? I don't play that game. Royal, my boss, doesn't allow it, and I don't operate that way anyway."

"You strike me as someone who does what you want."

"Oh?" A short laugh escapes my throat. "I guess. I take care of myself, that's what I do. And the community around here, well, they're more into hookups. One night. Not much talk if you know what I mean. I want more substance."

Nic rubs his hand on his leg, looking down. "I'm not sure I can give you that."

My chest knots. "What?" I let out a shallow breath.

"There are things about me. Well, things you don't know, can't know. I don't even live here."

"Are you saying you want to spend time with me, but you'll eventually leave?"

"Not eventually. I'm here for only another eleven days."

"So this place." I glance around at all the decorations. Obviously, the cabin came furnished, but most likely not with all the lights and knickknacks and a fully decked out tree. "You rented it and did all this just for a short time?"

Nic nods.

My heart aches. My every limb feels weighted as if gravity has increased in the last few seconds. Yet, I want to be with this man. I want to feel his arms around me and his lips on mine again. If I allow just that, and sex, and hold the rest of myself back, maybe I won't get attached.

But who am I kidding? Any relationship that lasts longer than three days, I get attached. It's been my habit.

But every part of me does not want to end this here, does not want to let this man go. Already, my mind is spinning plans to take a few personal days off work. I want to spend as much time with Nic, even if it is temporary.

I already want more. How do I say it without looking like a fool?

Everything is hot and sort of misty. The lights compete to blind me. It is as if I've entered a dream where everything is hazy but beautiful and safe. The dream contains so much of what I've wanted in my life. A handsome older man, warmth, sizzling feelings inside me of utter desire and trust.

Trust. That's a big word. *He'll hurt you.* The voice in my head comes from reason, but if I were being reasonable, I would never have driven by Nic's cabin at one in the morning.

"Well? Now that I've told you I may not be everything you wish for, what do you think?" Nic asks.

"I'm thinking I'm up for it." I reach out and place my palm over his hand. "Yes, I want to spend time with you while you are here."

It'll hurt when he leaves. Maybe badly. But I can't say no to this man. I just can't.

Nic turns his hand up and clasps mine. A surge of adrenaline rushes through my veins. My cock throbs.

That's it. There's nothing I can do now. I'm caught. I'm hooked by this Santa daddy who makes me feel like Christmas magic really exists, who exudes a sort of trust and safety. This man who calls deer his friends is someone I want to get to know better. Even if he's leaving in eleven days.

Our heads move toward each other. His lips brush first the corner of my mouth, then my cheek. Our surroundings tilt. Or I do. I'm not sure which way is up, or what is reality right now except for this man before me. This man who seems to want me as much as I want him.

I lift my chin so our mouths can meet. I open to him and his lips are velvet against mine, against my curious tongue. His strong arms come around me. Then I am lost to him.

Nic pulls back a fraction. "The things I want to do to you."

"I want them all."

This time the kiss is fiercer. Nic's hands run up and down my back, tight and hot, the fingers curving and lightly digging in. I wrap my own arms beneath his, around his waist. The muscles of his back are rock hard; he's solid as I lock in my embrace. I move closer to him until our chests touch. I bring my legs up and now I'm practically sitting in his lap.

Our tongues meet. Nic runs his hand up my neck and into my hair, pulling my head closer to his. His fingers comb through my hair, the tips lightly scratching at my scalp. Hot swirls of desire wash over me.

A force we cannot control comes over us and suddenly Nic pulls me fully onto his lap just as I lift myself to climb over him. Everything is pressed together now. My legs are bent on either side of Nic's thighs. My chest heaves.

With a smooth motion, Nic moves his arms underneath mine and stands. My legs wrap around him and his hands cup my ass as he lifts me.

"Yes!" I breathe this one word into him.

He doesn't have to say a word. I know he's taking me into his bedroom.

Left behind: warm fire, cocoa, no regrets.

Nic places me gently onto his bed. I lift my head and look around.

The walls are natural wood, varnished. The ceiling is dark and high beamed. The only light comes from a lamp with a base shaped like a Christmas tree.

I have a truly inconsequential thought: *He brought a lamp with him for the two weeks he's in town?*

But that has nothing to do with what's important. What's right in front of me.

Nic says, "May I unwrap you?"

Strange words for an awesome request. "Yes."

"Lie still."

"I don't know if I can be still," I reply.

"I'll help you if you have trouble." Nic starts unbuttoning my shirt.

"Oh? How will you do that?" I reach up to grasp his arms and he pushes my hands down to my sides, then finishes with the last button at the hem, his fingers moving right over my abdomen.

"I will remind you. At first."

"At first?"

"Sit up a little now," he says with a soft smile.

As I lift myself up he pulls the shirt up, then begins to pull it off my left arm. He's graceful and intent on the job, looking more at the shirt than at me. I puff my chest out a little.

When Nic holds my shirt, he says, "Lie back down."

My entire body trembles at those words. I try to relax but my muscles are tense with longing. I'm hungry. For this. For him.

Out the corner of my eye, in the dim lamplight, I watch Nic neatly fold my shirt and put it on the top of the dresser. He turns toward me and the edge of the light catches his eyes and makes them spark.

I lean back and put my hands behind my head. Waiting.

Nic says, "Hands at your sides."

*Really?* I obey without question. My fingers curve into loose fists. I trust him, but I'm taut with need, and maybe a little shyness since this is our first time.

Nic gets into the bed beside me, balancing on his hip and with one hand over my body and pressed to the mattress by my waist. He leans over me and his gold-brown hair glistens.

I can see the depths of dark blue in his eyes now, like looking into an ocean without end, no land in sight. His lips are pink like carnations and soft as they part a fraction. Just a fraction. Not enough to see his teeth or tongue.

His cheeks are smooth as if freshly shaved, the skin a natural tan hue, smooth with deeper lines around the mouth. His eyes crinkle, but from joy, not age.

Though he looks mature, anywhere between thirty and forty, I sense from him an even deeper tie with time. Why I think that, I haven't a clue. Weird thoughts often come to me when I am in the throes of arousal. When I am ready to make love with a man who strokes every flame within me.

Slowly, his free hand comes up and touches, just the fingertips, lightly on my chest. It moves between my pecs where the skin is paler. Where he touches, the skin seems to vibrate.

I sigh and close my eyes half-way so I can bask but still look at him. His intensity, the way his muscles contract beneath his red shirt, how he moves his head closer to mine as if to kiss me again.

Except, he doesn't. His fingers keep trailing slowly, over my diaphragm, down one side of my ribcage. My nipples are pebbles now, they are so hard. The warmth of him permeates my every pore.

I squirm.

"Lie still," he says. A rumble from deep in his lungs.

I already love him because this man likes to take charge. I've been waiting for that sort of guy. My whole life, I think.

My cock presses to my tight jeans with an ache I love to feel but haven't been chasing lately because everyone is so fucking boring. So fucking young and vapid. I want release but Nic appears to be the sort who doesn't like to rush.

Good. I need that in my life. I want that in my life.

I try to see his pants, center my gaze there, but his hand is in the way. Is there a bulge? Is he as desperate as I am?

I bend my knee to give myself more room in my pants.

Nic says, "Still. Be still my beautiful Angel. Do you not listen?"

"I can't. You're driving me crazy."

"That's the point, isn't it?"

I bite hard on my lower lip as I nod. But then I feel like begging. "Kiss me again, please?"

Nic smiles, lowers his head, and kisses my forehead.

I make a strangled sound of frustration.

He laughs. The laugh pours over me like liquid warmth. From just that, I think I might actually come in my pants.

His hand continues to touch me, roving all the way to my waistband, slightly tickling, then moving upward again. His forefinger stumbles over my right nipple, which is hard and sensitive. I gasp.

Without warning, Nic leans down and licks it. I melt into the mattress. My hips lift without my—or Nic's—permission.

He takes his mouth away. "You cannot seem to follow even the simplest direction."

"Tell that to my boss." Though, in fact, I am a good worker and do everything Royal tells me to do.

Nic gives a little pat—not a smack, not a hit, just a pat—to my stomach and lowers his head. This time he takes the nipple into his mouth and lightly sucks.

My fingers become tight fists. My toes curl in my boots, which I am still wearing, damn it. My sphincter throbs.

I want to reach up and hug him closer to me. But he told me not to move. I want to thrust up, beg him to unzip my jeans. Instead, I groan out all my wishes in unintelligible sounds.

Nic brushes me with the side of his head and that soft hair nestles against my chin.

My hand comes up all on its own. I swear I didn't think of moving it. I grip Nic's shoulder.

Nic moves back and shakes his head. "Now you've done it."

"What?"

"I gave you so many chances."

My face flushes. "And?" Could I hope for what I think he might be implying?

Nic simply raises an eyebrow.

I decide I'll go for it. Break the barrier, so to speak, on what looks to be leading toward the kind of play I can get into. "Are you going to punish me? Daddy?"

For a long time, Nic stares at me. Silent. Unmoving. I start to get scared he is going to toss me off the bed. Or worse. Hurl me out into the freezing night never to see me again.

But Nic does neither. He starts to unbutton his own shirt. I watch without moving—see, I can be good—as he shrugs it off his arms revealing a muscular chest and flat, broad shoulders, rippled abs. His tanned skin gleams, rises and swells in all the right places. He has a bit of gold shimmering on his chest, hair like gilt. His stomach and waist taper nicely toward his narrow hips.

He gets up and folds his shirt as he did with mine and sets it on the dresser. I get a great view of his magnificent, wide back. He wears black trousers that are belted tight, and his skin is so hard and firm it barely dimples where the belt wraps him.

He turns. "Strip," he orders.

"I can move?"

"Don't be cute."

"But I am cute."

His eyebrows go up. "So you say. Show me."

Oh, this is wonderful. I want this guy in any way. I want him to do everything to me.

I sit up and undo the laces on my boots. I kick them off, not caring where they go, and strip off my socks. Then I undo the top button on my jeans. I unzip them. It's a relief as I already feel my cock expand with new freedom. I lean back on my elbows, lift my hips and shove my jeans and underwear down all in one motion.

I lean over to get the garments off my feet and let them drop to the floor. As I bend, I am hiding myself. Shadowing with my arms and knees. My cock is fully stiff now, tapping my belly. The air is cool against the tip, though Nic's bedroom is quite warm.

Slowly, I rise, my upper body coming up.

Nic watches me, his gaze focused and still.

I move until I am stretched out on my back, my head at the pillows, my hands at my sides. I shiver, but not because I'm cold. My cock juts out from my body and the weight of it lets it rest on my abdomen near my right hip.

Nic walks toward me until he's at the side of the bed. He lets out a long breath.

"You're lovely, you know."

I do know. But I still flush all over.

"Perfect," he adds.

I bask in the compliments. I want him to touch me, but he doesn't.

Nic says, "Turn over."

My eyes widen. I don't question, though. I move until I'm on my stomach.

"If you don't mind, on your knees, head down."

"I don't mind," I hear myself say.

My heart pounds. My ass is in the air. I am so aroused the edge of my vision is gray with little specks darting about.

My head is turned, facing Nic, but he moves outside my vision. I think I hear him at the foot of the bed. Then I feel the bed move, and the weight of his knee on the mattress alongside me.

"Part your knees a bit," Nic says.

I quiver. My cock waves between my legs. "Is this the punishment?"

"It is. Unless--"

"I know I was a bad boy," I say quickly. Perhaps a little too eager.

"Not bad at all," Nic replies. "Just a bit naughty."

I grin into the pillow.

"Do you have a safe word?" Nic asks quietly.

Fuck. Do I need one? "Moonlight."

When I was sixteen and realized I was completely gay and my fantasies drove me toward any sexual idea and all kinds of porn, I made a list of words. Safe words. It seemed deeply and truly important to me at the time, and not just any word would do. I was a teenager. I liked the drama of making handwritten lists, scribbling hard with my pencil while my tongue worried at my bottom lip.

On that list I had the usual sort of ordinary safe words: red, redlight, redbird. But I wanted to be different. Unique. I put cutesy words on the list. Like unicorn and rainbow. I wrote down tough boy words like dinosaur and gangster. Then I went toward the more poetic.

I love night. I'm sort of big on sci fi and fantasy. So I went in that direction. Some words seem awkward or might be hard to remember in the heat of the moment. I settled on moonlight because it is my favorite kind of light since you can only see it at night.

My word prompts a touch. Warm palm. Left buttock. Barely a stroke.

"Good," Nic says. "I like that word."

I hear the sound, the rap of skin on skin hitting before I feel the sensation travel my body. The single spank leaves me momentarily dazed, and the tip of my cock drips as the shaft seems to expand more than ever.

Just as I am assessing all the sensations, another spank impacts my right cheek.

I have wanted this. Secretly craved it. From age sixteen on. But I never met anyone who actually delivered. They would talk. Laugh. Tempt and tease but when it came down to the game of spanking, or other such play, they had no will to continue. They just wanted to fuck. They'd get themselves off. Then leave. That was my experience so far.

Nic is older and more graceful. More thoughtful. At the third spank, which rattles me to my balls, I feel myself open to Nic and his personality. To the idea of a man who might take me, control me, let me escape from my own life of utter and complete control and leave it behind. For these moments. For these times.

"I've been very naughty!" I say through gritted teeth.

"Then take your punishment like big boy," Nic replies.

"Yes, Daddy."

Everything opens inside me. Heart, soul, core. Balls aching for release. Ass wiggling as if begging to be filled.

50

My body gives off heat as if I'm in a fever. I have no shame, but I am unsure. Because this happiness is so great and it's going to end. It's finite.

More spanks. Harder each time.

My eyes well. I rub my face deeper into the pillow. It's not the pain. It's the idea that I'll be left behind that gets me.

"Harder!" I say into the pillow. I want to feel it all. If I only have eleven days, I want it mean, hard, fast, slow, soft, gentle, agonizing, and real.

My cock, heavy and rigid, pushes into the bedspread. I resist the urge to thrust, to come. I won't come until Nic says it's okay. I hope with all my heart that's the game he's playing, because I want it. In fact, I want it as more than a game. I want it for real.

Nic spanks hard and fast now.

"Daddy, I'll be good." My voice holds a hint of a whimper.

"I know you will, sweet boy," comes the answer.

Thrills race through me.

"But you need to learn," Nic continues. "This is for your own good."

*Fuck, yes it is.*

Ten more thwaps. His own hands must be aching as well. Then I feel him move over me. He's balanced on his hands, so his entire weight doesn't push onto me, but he's warm, and his naked chest touches my back as his still-clad hips push against my ass.

"My beautiful boy, you were very good to take your punishment so well."

"Thank you, Daddy." Again, my eyes sting. This is what I've been wanting. Needing.

He rises up. "Turn over now, sweet Angelbaby," he says.

His body is very close. I maneuver myself onto my side, then lie back. My ass burns, even the smooth bedcovers sting as they cushion me. Nic hovers and his pupils are big, obscuring all the dark blue of his irises. His mouth is open, his bottom lip shiny as if he just licked it.

I want to feel those lips, his kisses. I want them everywhere, all over, all the time.

"Legs spread, please."

I comply. I blink upward. "Yes, Daddy."

Nic positions himself between my legs. I watch him gaze at me, up and down my body. His view lingers on my cock and his naked chest rises and falls a little faster. At that response from him, pre-cum gushes out of me and drips onto my abdomen.

"You will stay very still now, won't you, baby?" Nic asks.

"Yes, Daddy."

"You've learned your lesson, haven't you?"

"I truly have, Daddy." My ass is hot and aching. My eyes roll back in pleasure.

"Let me see, then," he says mysteriously.

He lets his hand trail over my pecs again, and my nipples. I hold myself very still.

"If you move again," Nic says, "restraints may be needed. But I don't have them with me at the moment."

"I'll try to be good, Daddy." Restraints? I am so into this! And he's so caring. I've wanted someone to care like that for so long.

Nic now uses both hands to smooth his way down my chest and stomach. He trails them on either side of my flushed and engorged cock and flattens them down my thighs. His biceps bunch. His chest muscles slither under his fine, tan skin.

Up and down my thighs his hands go, massaging, warming. My cock jumps. But it doesn't count. I haven't moved. I'm ready to defend myself if need be on that point.

Nic does not react or judge. His thumbs delve to the insides of my thighs. They reach my balls, exposed and drawn tight with need. His fingers gently caress them. I grit my teeth. The thumbs circle the drawn up flesh, one on each ball, and the ache inside me widens. Now the fingers brush the base of my shaft. I imagine their heat circling, squeezing, milking.

But Nic is patient and so I must be patient, too.

I let out a moan. I am allowed to make noise, am I not?

"Good boy."

That answers that question.

"Now," says Nic. "Hold very still while I take care of my baby boy. You've been naughty but you took your punishment. But this looks like a sorry state you're in right now."

I am not sure what to say. Should I apologize? Should I agree and spur him on that yes, I'm naughty, and I can be naughtier? I've always wanted this, but it's not like I've done the daddy-boy game before. Nowhere but in my most private thoughts, that is.

"Hold very still for Daddy, all right?"

"I will."

"You're such a beautiful boy. Let Daddy take care of you."

Oh my. And finally

Nic goes with it and says everything I've ever dreamed of hearing. Words that heat me up past the boiling point, past what I've ever felt before.

"You're a naughty boy, and a bit messy. When you get stiff like that it will stay that way unless you let me help you."

I so need help. I'm going to explode in all the wrong ways if I don't get help.

"But," continues Nic, "there is a right way and wrong way. My way is the right way."

"Always, Daddy."

"You must be very still. You mustn't move."

"Yes, sir, Daddy."

"First, let's clean you a little." Then he takes my cock, holds it straight up, bends his head and licks expertly all around the head.

My entire body stiffens at the sensation. The top of my head feels like it comes off. My vision goes blurred and dark as my eyes roll up.

The tongue continues to lick me all over.

Nic says, "You need a good thorough cleaning."

He lets his tongue and sometimes his lips trail up and down the sides of my shaft. Then the tongue keeps licking away at the wet tip. My balls squirm. Everything is close. So close. But he edges me just right so I don't spill over. Yet.

Nic pulls back. "Such a naughty boy but you're doing to well."

"I want to be good, Daddy."

"You're getting there."

He lowers his heads and takes the tip of my cock into his mouth and lightly suckles.

"Oh Daddy! That feels so good. I don't know if I can hold back."

"You don't have to hold back for Daddy now." Nic rubs my shaft up and down, palm curved, fingers curled.

"Oh!"

"It's all right. I'm going to suck you now so you can come. All right baby boy?"

"Oh. Wow. It's okay then?"

"Yes. You need to come now. Daddy says it's okay."

"And it's not too messy and naughty?"

"It's very messy and naughty. But you need it. You've been so very bad, but you need it."

I love our dialog. I want it to be this way between us always. But I'll take the short term, too. It's just too fun.

Before I can say another word, Nic takes my cock into his mouth and sucks down on it, then up.

My fingers grip the bedspread until I think it might rip. My body and mind rise as one higher and higher toward the peak. The climax.

Nic's mouth sucks harder. I want to thrust but I remember his command not to move. Every part of me wants to please him, to obey him. This is my fantasy. To be worshipped, cared for. Babied. Loved.

I can let go now. No worry about slow nights with no tips when the blizzards hit. No worry about keeping my nice things, paying the bills, looking for something to fulfill me that I can never define. No worry about Royal frowning at me, or me sweeping snow and ice from the front door alcove in nothing but my leather pants and a bow tie.

I feel it deep in my bones. At the bottom of my spine. In the heat of my veins and the back of my throat. The eruption comes from every part of my being.

My cock throbs and I feel it. Feel the spurt as Nic continues to suck.

He drinks me through my orgasm. I've lost all sense but pleasure now, the ecstasy tossing me, turning me through a whiteness brighter than moonlight on snow. *Moonlight.* I certainly don't need to use that word right now.

When I come down, Nic is cradling me in his arms, kissing my forehead. I'm turned halfway onto my side. Nic has his hands under my bent knees and his other arm around my shoulders. My face is pressed to the crook of his neck. My arm is thrown over his naked stomach. He still wears his black pants.

"Are you okay?" Nic asks.

"Yes. I'm wonderful." I lift my head a little and look at him. "But what about you?"

54

"Let me take care of you first," he says, his lips pursing.

I kiss his neck, then his chin. He lets me, then rolls me to the side. I rock my head back and watch him climb over me. Before I can ascertain what's happening, he leans down, puts his arms under my shoulders and knees again, and lifts me.

I wrap my arms around his neck. "What are you doing?"

"Naughty, messy boy needs a bath."

Bathing fantasies have always been forefront in my mind. I've never told a soul.

Nic takes me to an adjoining bathroom where everything is adorned in white faux-fur. The toilet seat. The back of the toilet. The rug that is laid out in front of the tub.

Nic sets me on the closed lid of the toilet and starts the water running into the tub, testing it every few seconds. He glances up at me as he does so. His mouth curves. His brow lifts.

"Wouldn't want it too hot or cold for my baby boy."

I lift my legs and hug my knees to my chest.

When Nic is satisfied, he lets the water run and pours soap into the water. The scent of evergreen rises in the air. White bubbles begin to form in the water.

We say nothing to each other until the tub is full. Nic turns to me and holds out his arms. I lift myself into them and he holds me again, cradled to his chest, then slowly bends his knees and lowers me into the tub.

The water is hot but not burning and flows over my sore bottom and up over my legs. When my ass hits the floor of the tub, the water is waist deep.

Nic kneels and grabs a washcloth. He washes me, starting with my shoulders and working his way down.

Everything feels warm and safe. My mind is still reeling from such unguarded pleasure. To add to that, Nic begins to compliment me. He tells me how smart I am. How perfect. How much he loved bringing me to ecstasy. Then he confesses to me he hasn't met anyone in a very long time he felt secure enough to be with in this way.

"Me, either," I admit.

The cloth gently delves between my legs. I am enthralled and my cock springs to life again. I lean back in the hot water and groan as the bubbles frame my arms and bobbing knees in rivulets of white foam.

I look up at Nic's sparkling gaze. A hint of white teeth peek between his open lips. The bathroom light catches all the strands of gold in his hair and lights them up.

"I want to touch you, too," I say.

"Yes, my boy. Yes."

After he's done making me all tingly again, Nic rises. He points at the showerhead.

"Rinse off and join me in bed?"

"Yes, Daddy."

I want to bask in the luxury of all of this goodness. I want to hurry as well because Nic is waiting for me, and I can't wait to explore him.

Nic leaves me to finish rinsing. I stand and soapy water pours over my skin in sleek falls. I open the drain and turn on the overhead shower while the water spins away.

When I step into the warm bedroom wrapped in a towel, my hair still dripping on my shoulders, Nic has lit candles everywhere. Real wax ones, not electric. I never saw them at all when I first came in. If he gathered them from the living room, well then, he works fast.

He lounges on the bed, the covers up to his waist, his chest and broad shoulders golden in the flickers of light. He motions me to him. My body surges before I take one step.

This is no longer my secret. I want to stay with him for as long as he'll have me. I want to be with him again and again until I can't stay awake, until I can't walk or think.

I'm no fool, but I'm young and needy. Nic fills all the empty spaces, even those I never knew I had.

# Chapter Six

## Nic

I've never felt comfortable enough around anyone to act out my deepest, wildest fantasies—until Angel.

Now I watch him approach the bed, his hair drenched, his towel slung low on his slim hips. Everything I am wants to hold him, baby him, spoil him. This instinct in me to give is often overwhelming, but nothing like how I feel now, watching Angel drop the towel so I can see his entire body.

Unabashed, he climbs onto the bed on his knees and sits back on his heels. His chest is shiny with moisture. Beads of water cling to the ends of his locks. His eyes are big and wide, brows narrowed to accompany an almost sinister smile.

After everything I just did to him, for him, his young cock is thick and stiff between his thighs. Ready for more.

"Your hair is soaked," I observe.

"I'm sorry, Daddy. I didn't find a hair drier."

"It's all right. Next time, you ask me, all right?"

"Yes, sir."

I love that he's willing to play with me. I want him badly. I have never played in this way with anyone before, human or elf from my own realm. I've been afraid they might sense something off about me, and when I think this way, when I share myself as a daddy in this way, I become too attached. And too afraid they'll run away.

That very scenario is playing out now, but I put it out of my mind. I have eleven days to deal with the blowback of my decision to take Angel into my arms for a temporary affair. For now, who we are is all that matters. Daddy and boy. Eager to be with each other, together, entwined, connected.

Angel says, "Can I touch you, Daddy?"

I smile.

"Please?"

"Yes."

He reaches out to touch my chest, then he leans over me and his wet hair brushes my shoulder. He kisses me below the neck, between my pecs. My world turns inside out; it feels like he has me in a snare. This boy and his invisible butterfly net has no idea he's caught a fairy elf who flies. I don't have wings but I am a rare creature with a nature he can only imagine.

Slowly, this human enigma kisses down my body, pushing away the covers and revealing my hunger, my lust.

"Oh," he exclaims. "Oh."

He's quick to grasp my shaft. Quick at everything he wants. I let him because I've been waiting. Waiting so long. My cock is thick and full. The ache of it extends to my back and my limbs. My lungs heave. My stomach flutters.

Angel licks the head of my cock with tentative darts of his tongue.

"That's it, baby boy. That's absolutely perfect."

"You are perfect," he replies. Then sucks on the tip.

My head tilts back on the pillows and bangs against the wall. The room turns to swirls and shapes of color and shadow mixing until I can't make anything out. I close my eyes and focus only on what Angel is doing.

The boy knows. He knows. How to be very very naughty. His mouth goes down a little more with each stroke up and he has a strong suck. My balls draw up.

When Angel takes me to the hilt, I hold my breath. He goes up and down, letting the head of my cock nestle in the back of his throat.

I can't control my body's squirm. He's a talented little thing and though I might have had a good time teaching him how to do this if he were inexperienced, in the moment I'm glad I don't have to say a word. I can lie back, relax and enjoy.

But I do speak. Words escape my mind and mouth.

"Good boy."

"That's it, baby."

"Oh, Daddy loves that mouth."

Usually I have never spoken such things. Not aloud. Only in my deepest, secret thoughts have I ever entertained such games. My lovers from the past have been straightforward, sweet, but unimaginative. None spoke even a dirty word to me.

Angel is not intimidated. He doesn't know who I truly am.

58

His wet hair dangles against my thighs. I love the contrast of cool and damp, hot and wet. Angel moves his head, twists his mouth. I cannot hold back.

"Sweet boy, oh, Angelbaby, you are so naughty. I am going to come."

He does not move away. Some of my distant past lovers did not enjoy drinking the essence of love. But Angel bears down and sucks harder and that's the end of me.

I come in a blast of sheer and wild abandon, my cock spasming. He swallows me and keeps swallowing until the orgasm fades.

I reach down and pull him up my body and into my arms. We kiss and I can taste myself upon his lips: tart and autumnal. Elfin. It would simply be sweet to him compared to tasting another human. Sweet. Lightly spiced, like pumpkins ripening in an ancient field of long-haired grass.

We lose ourselves in each other. Again and again. The still-dark early hours of the morning come and go. We doze in each other's arms. He whispers Daddy in my ear as he settles. His head rests on my shoulder. His unruly blond hair tickles my chin. Our legs tangle together.

I wake and grab my phone from the nightstand to check the time. It's late morning, which does not surprise me. We wore each other out.

Angel sleeps like the sweet boy he is, curled onto his side pushing up against me, knees bent, hands clasped at his chest. In this moment, he looks innocent and unassuming, but I do not mistake this reality. Angel is a dynamo. He knows what he wants and he has stolen my heart.

Carefully, I moved the covers back and push my legs over the side of the bed. I try not to jiggle the mattress as I rise. After a trip to the bathroom, I go to my kitchen and fix a tray.

I'm not sure what he likes, so breakfast consists of eggs and toast with pancakes on the side. I am used to eating a lot of sweets and carbs. I can handle them. Humans, I know, must eat a little less than that, but Angel is too young to worry about that, and after our all night antics, carbs and sugar will bring him back to life.

I add some hot tea and orange juice to the tray.

When I enter the bedroom and set the tray at the edge of the bed, Angel moves, waking up. He rubs his eyes. He glances about the room, then to the side, no doubt looking for me.

"I brought breakfast," I say.

He lifts his head and as he sees me his entire face lights up with a smile.

"Hungry?"

"Starving," he replies. "And I have to pee."

Later, we eat breakfast in bed, side by side.

"Can we stay in bed all day, Daddy?"

His voice flows over me, thick and sated with the meal. He leans back and his eyelids close.

"If that's what you wish."

"I wish."

We have another nap. I wake with Angel kissing and licking at my left nipple. My cock is already hard. Ready.

Angel looks at me with a smile.

I do know what he is thinking. I've thought the same thing. His eyes ask the question. When am I going to take him?

"I think I need to be punished again, Daddy," he says with a tilt of his head and not an ounce of remorse.

"Oh? Why?"

"Because I have very naughty thoughts."

I laugh and he joins in. Then we're kissing as if the world around us has ended, or perhaps never even existed. It's just the two of us and warm limbs wrapping around each other. I feel as if my essence is sinking into him, and his into me.

I don't recall ever feeling more joined to another. We've been on one date. We've met a total of three times counting this entire night. Can it be possible I am falling in love already?

I discount nothing as impossible. There are invisible worlds all around. All one world, but individually divided. My presence here on the human world is proof of that. But love at first sight? Attraction, surely. An affinity for each other. Matching chemistry where it counts. But love is an elusive definition to pin down. Both simple and many-layered at the same time. Does one actually *fall* into it?

Yet that is exactly what I am experiencing. Last night. Now.

"I want you," Angel whispers. "In me."

Seductive. Enticing. My naughty boy.

"On your hands and knees," I command.

He obeys without hesitation.

The beauty of him. The sweet leanness of his young body, the slender muscles rippling beneath his skin. I touch the small of his back. My hand trails over the taut and rounded globes of his ass. Smooth and hot to the touch. But I can make it hotter. I want to make it hotter.

I am already overwhelmed with desire, my body craving his, but I can wait just a little longer.

I spank him hard, and the skin of his buttocks ripples. I don't go all out as I did hours ago. Just enough to make his skin pink and warm, warmer. Enough to make him groan and stretch himself upward in wordless invitation.

"Imp," I say.

The world is not ready for this gift. I am not ready on deeper levels that scare me, that make me want to keep him as mine when that would be impossible being who I am. But I am ready on one level. And I can no longer wait.

I reach for the lube, pouring generous amounts into my palm and on my fingers. My thumb and forefinger track from the small of his back down the crack of his ass. My other hand grabs his left cheek.

He bends just right and his own hand goes back to his right cheek and spreads it for me. He opens to me until everything is revealed. His pucker is shaved and very pink.

My cock waves as if to remind me this is what it wants. As if I don't already have plans. As if I already don't know what I'm doing.

I tease the pucker and it tightens beneath my touch. I rub lightly and it relaxes. At that moment, I insert my middle finger, gently wiggling it to open him there. I hear him sigh.

He's gorgeous. Irresistible. My sweet boy.

I try to take my time, but it's been a long time for me. I know how to do this, but patience has left me behind in its static wake.

I insert a second finger and he takes it without complaint. I push in and out of him, watching him open to me, watching how my fingers disappear and reappear again.

He's hot inside. Slick with the lube on my fingers, but I can see he needs more.

I grab more lube, squirt it on him and on my cock. I spread him. I work it into him. Then my hands leave him for a moment as I quickly work it onto my cock.

Then with a start, something occurs to me that I had never had to think of before. Will he want me to use protection? I am immortal, immune to disease. Not a carrier. How can I convey that he is safe?

He turns his head to look at me, eyebrows raised. "I have condoms in my car." He makes a sheepish face.

Thinking quickly, I say, "I've recently been tested." It's a lie, but not a harmful one. I don't need any test.

"Me, too," he says. "But, you know, they always warn not to take that at face value."

I nod; my words clog in my throat, but I push them out. "I will stop, then."

"No, please. Daddy. Please. I want you."

A risk-taker. That's what he is. But also, like me, more caught up in the moment than anything else. It happens. To everyone, I figure.

"I promise you, I am safe."

"I believe you," he says, his eyes big and shining, the whites glowing. "Please. I want you. I want you in me. Now."

"Boys never tell their daddies what to do."

"No." He bows his head beneath his shoulder which is raised above his elbow. "But they do beg for what they want. A lot."

My laugh echoes off the walls.

"You have the best laugh, Daddy," he says.

I prod him in the ass with my finger and he drops his head with a strangled sound. "Please. Please. Now."

I grab myself and brush the tip of my wet cock across his sleek hole. It's so sensitive and my need turns my skin to fire all over.

"Take me bare, Daddy."

He knows just what to say to send me over the edge. "You are such a bad boy."

"I know."

I push with the head of my cock. There is resistance at first, not his fault. No one's fault. Just the way the body works. Gripping myself more firmly, I push with my hips. Angel pushes back. Then gives out a yelp as the head breaches him. I hold back, waiting for him to relax, but he's so hot and tight and I need. I need. I need to thrust.

Angel wiggles his hips. Slowly, I move forward. I watch my cock sink into him, the skin of it sliding against the pink rim, slipping further inside him. It's like a squeezing hug on the most sensitive part of my body. I want to move. I want to buck. But when I'm all the way in, I hold myself as still as possible.

"Oh, Daddy, oh. It's so big. I can feel it. It stretches me. Is it in all the way?"

"Yes, boy. My baby, it's all the way inside you. You have taken it very well." This sort of talk riles me up. I can't help it. He's saying all the words I never thought another person would ever say to me. And I get to respond in ways I've only dreamed.

"Oh, I love it. It's so big. I feel like you're inside me. I mean, with more than just you big, giant, hard, swollen—ugh!"

As he is talking his dirty talk, there is no more control. I love it too much. I'm going to come too soon if I don't shut him up, so before he finishes his sentence I pull out and push back in, then out again keeping just the tip inside him.

"More, Daddy. More."

I feel the glide of the lube easing my passage with each thrust. It gets easier as we go and soon I'm slipping and thrusting in and out and we are fucking—no, this is more than that. We're making love. What is happening between us can only be that, making love, both of us moaning to wake the very walls of this cabin. Can sound collapse structure? I don't know. Maybe we'll find out.

I get a rhythm going that is pleasurable but I won't last long. And by the sounds Angel makes, he's not going to last, either.

"Oh, oh, Daddy, slower. Please! I don't want to come just yet. I want this to last forever."

"Maybe not forever, baby boy."

"Can I face you? Can I see you, Daddy?"

It means pulling out. I hate to leave his warmth, but how can I deny my boy? Even in my deepest, wildest fantasies, I cannot deny the faceless boy that has populated all my scripts. But this one has a face. A gorgeous face. And I would give him anything in this moment. Anything at all.

I pull out with a slick pop.

Angel turns beneath me, his cock bobbing before me. As he settles onto his back, I lean down and give the head a lick.

"Oh, please. Please put it back in." He spreads his legs, a wanton child, and uses his hands to pull his knees up to his chest.

I grab my throbbing member and push it into him. It's smooth and easy this time. It goes right to the hilt and I'm moving again, slow at first, then faster, watching myself appear and disappear inside him.

The lube offers up a sweet but whispery slick sound. I don't know how to stop as I stare into Angel's beautiful eyes. His mouth is open, his white teeth gritted, his eyelids half-closed. His cheeks are rosy with exertion and ecstasy. His chest, below his bent knees, rises and falls with his quick breaths.

I am balanced now on my hands, one on either side of him at his waist. But now, as I fuck into him in rapid succession, I push my hands underneath him. I pull him up and he responds immediately by lifting his legs further and wrapping them around my waist. I pull him up and to me until our chests are touching and he's seated in my lap. I feel his hard cock against my stomach.

I move in and out of him, my face nuzzling the side of his neck. He grabs my shoulders and we're like one being now, joined together in complete abandon.

"Oh, sweet boy, I can't hold back."

"Don't hold back, Daddy." His voice purrs in my ear. "Come inside me."

I push harder inside him, lifting up and pushing in again. I try to rub his cock against my stomach as well, but mostly I focus on holding him tight to me. Moving my hips. Three more times and that's it. I'm exploding into him, the bursts jerking through my body. The orgasm takes me up and up, through the ceiling, out among the clouds and moon and stars.

It feels like a long time before I come down, and I find myself lying on top of him, still hard inside him. A sticky wetness mingles on both our chests letting me know he has come, too.

My mouth is on his chin. His is near my ear. Our breaths are loud in the quiet room. The sweat of our bodies combines as if we have melted into each other.

We rest. Or maybe we pass out. I am not quite sure which. But it doesn't matter. I have him. He has me. For now.

# Chapter Seven

## Angel

Nic wakes just enough to pull the covers over us. He gently eases me onto my side but I don't want to let go. My arms close tighter around him.

"It's all right, baby. Hold on tight."

I bury my face in his chest, then say, "When can we do that again?"

"Behave yourself," he says. But I can hear his voice is a bit breathless. He wants me again. It's like last night when we couldn't stop touching, embracing, exploring. Hands, fingers, mouths everywhere. All night long.

His warm room. His soft bed. I never want to leave. It's a stupid kid thought. Immature. But it's pure truth. And that truth hits me with a lot of twinges in deep places that are rarely touched. In fact, Nic is the first to make me feel this way.

Others, well, they've come and gone and for a reason. We weren't compatible. We were too young. We didn't feel comfortable emotionally to connect further than shallow sex where the mechanics seemed more important than any feelings.

I have strong desires within me, but I've never had them awakened so thoroughly until now.

True to Nic's word, we stay in bed all day. By evening, he has drawn another bath for me. He bathes me with gentle care, asking after me, making sure every inch of me is clean and unharmed. He gets into the tub with me after adding more hot water, and hugs me, my back to his chest, holding me to him tight enough that I can feel the beat of his heart.

Something about him is so special. Like my mind knows a secret it wants to tell me but can't find the context, let alone the words. But he strikes me as different and unique, more than a mysterious rich man who runs a toy company and might like Christmas a little too much.

He plays with me in the tub like a man who has just found a new toy and can't stop touching it. He puts his hand over my thighs and between my legs, drawing my cock up out of the water, his fingers curving around it and squeezing, milking.

I've come so many times, I simply lie back on his chest and enjoy the softness, the soapiness of his hand on my skin. I expect nothing more, until my cock hardens. The tip swells bigger as his hand moves up, tightening around the head. It reddens.

A few more tugs and I'm coming hard, spraying upward in arcs to land on the bubbles that crowd the surface of the bath water.

I cry out, my head lolling on Nic's broad chest.

For the entire day I feel as if I am in some sort of holiday wonderland. The house is full of lights and wonderful scents and food. The very air is tinged with a kind of static, a magic electricity that fills me up. When I'm not with Nic, I'm wandering about the cabin peering at every decoration and knickknack, or eating Nic's fabulous baked goods.

We lounge on the plush couch together. We make love on the fuzzy rug before a crackling fire.

People my age are usually on their phones in a constant daze, but I never once glance at mine. I only know what time it is because there is a digital clock by the bed, and a wall clock shaped like a snowflake over the mantel.

Now I'm curled on Nic's lap and we're watching a movie. He holds me and I doze, missing most of the action.

I wake and Nic is gone, a blanket covering me where I am sprawled on the couch. I get up and peer out the front window, parting the flannel plaid curtains. It's dark out but the moon is up making the snow beyond his porch glow. Beyond that I see the little road and it's like all that out there is another life. Someone else's life. I never want to leave this cabin.

But as I glance at the clock, I realize I have to go home some time. Tomorrow night I have a shift at Prancer's. If I don't show, I could get fired. We aren't some big corporation. We get five personal days a year. Sick leave is not paid.

I am tempted to take my five days and spend them with Nic. Would he want me for that long? Would he let me stay here? Of course, people have relationships *and* work. One does not exclusively cut out the other.

Nic comes up behind me and puts his hands on my naked waist.

"Anything interesting out there?" he asks.

"I don't see the deer yet."

"They'll be around. Want to help me feed them?"

"Yes!"

We bundle up. Nic dresses me like I'm a child who cannot dress himself. I love being taken care of this way.

We go out into the cold and the snow. Nic lets me carry the red bag of corn. He has a smaller bag of dried berries. We spread them on the white snow in the moonlight and wait. It doesn't take long.

First the deer appear as shadows slowly encroaching on Nic's property. When they move closer their features grow distinct. Golden brown bodies. Long faces with big dark eyes. Racks of antlers. Spindly long legs. They surround us. First three, then four. Then a dozen.

We don't move. We watch side by side as they come forward and begin to feed. They are so close I can feel the warmth of their bodies and see their breath from clouds by their little wet black noses.

Slowly, Nic reaches out with one ungloved hand and presses it to the back of one of the deer. The deer pauses in his feast, then resumes unafraid. Nic runs his hand down the animal's soft pelt.

I'm amazed. These are wild animals. They have lived here in these woods forever, hunted, bred to not trust humans. It's as if Nic has put a spell on the entire herd.

Nic motions for me to try. I reach out to a deer and it flinches.

Nic whispers, "Close your eyes. Let all your barriers down. Let them feel the core heart of you. Let them see your peaceful intent."

I cannot say enough how much I now love this man.

I reach out again and shut my eyes against the stars and moon, against the brilliant snow reflecting light everywhere from the road to the woods behind the cabin. I breathe in and the air goes through my body like a shiver. My lungs are over the first shocks of nighttime cold. My body, once tense, now releases all my pent up energy from the cold. I let my love for Nic flow over me.

I feel the softness of the pelt on my palm, and open my eyes. The deer is allowing this. She's letting me pet her. She is warm and alive and I'm making contact with her. Touching her.

Everywhere Nic goes, magic extends outward from him. Everything he touches, including myself, seems to bloom. Deer are drawn to him. As am I. I may not be a wild creature, but I have been, in a sense, lost in the woods. Lost in my own material world where more substance is craved but rarely attained.

After a while the cold begins to pierce my parka. We head back inside, our boots crunching the snow, the deer crunching their meal behind us.

"That was wonderful!"

The door closes behind me. The fire laps at the hearth. The warmth of the cabin hits me like a blast and my face instantly flushes.

Nic pulls my parka and scarf off me, then carries me to the bedroom and slowly, with attentive and loving affection, disrobes me.

We're both quite exhausted after our long day together, but we still have the energy to kiss and cuddle.

I fall to sleep in Nic's warm arms, whispering "Daddy" in his ear.

*

The sun is late upon the snow, making it pink. The days are shorter and shorter now.

"I can stay the day but I have to work at five."

Nic nods. "I know."

We've spent two glorious nights together. We now know every inch of each other's bodies.

We have a late lunch in front of the TV. I glance at the tree in the corner where the lights are set to chase each other around the pine branches, changing color from purple to blue to green to red.

Bright presents lie under the tree. I would swear they weren't there before.

"What are those for?" I point at the brightly wrapped packages.

"They are presents."

"Yes, but why? You're the only one who lives here."

"Christmas trees need presents underneath them, don't they?" Nic says.

"I guess." But I know they weren't there when I arrived in the middle of the night two nights ago. I sigh.

Nic ruffles my unbrushed hair. "Boys like surprises, yes?"

I make a scrunched up face at him. "Sometimes."

"Maybe you'll get one come Christmas."

68

I don't smile because I know I won't be here in this cabin for Christmas. I've been counting the days. Nic leaves in nine. He's been honest about that. It was stated that this affair between us would be temporary. No one has said a word otherwise.

I try not to be sad about it. It is what it is. But my heart aches. I have so fallen for this guy.

As if sensing the change in my mood, Nic nuzzles me. His hands stroke down my back.

Lunch is over. Eaten. Put aside.

I curl tightly into him and he holds me as I try to block my feelings about the future and simply bask in the now.

Too soon the afternoon is over.

I shower and get myself dressed. Nic does not intrude.

When I am ready to leave, he hands me a bag of goodies wrapped with a red bow.

"Will you return after your shift?" he asks.

This is the first time he's offered. I had been too tense to ask.

"Yes! I'll just go by my condo and collect a few things." Nic made sure I had everything, though, including my own toothbrush. I want more clothes, though I haven't been wearing them much. Just in case we decide to go out.

\*

"Angelbaby, you look rode hard and put away wet," Royal comments as I emerge from the back room in my leathers, my red bowtie, my fancy black boots and nothing else.

I spent a long time with the glitter in my hair and on my chest getting it just right.

"I look awesome," I curtly reply.

Royal's comment is unwarranted. Anyway, how can he know anything?

"Your eyes are lit up. Maybe it's the dark circles beneath them."

I know he's teasing, but I'm uneasy. Throughout the evening I keep checking my face in the garish lighting of the bathroom mirror.

It's a clear night, though icy. But men show up for Wednesday night twofers. They get their first two drinks for the price of one. It has me running back and forth from the bar to the tables for hours.

Despite fighting off flirtatious customers, I get great tips. Not once does Royal make me clear the ice from the foyer. He makes the newer guy, Desithekid do it.

All night, all I can think about is Nic. What he has done to me. What he is doing while I'm not there.

One o'clock cannot come quickly enough. I'm not closing tonight, so I don't need to stay until two, for which I am grateful.

I change into my jeans, stuff my tips in my small backpack, sling it over my shoulder and am out of there.

I drive to my condo to pack some things. The streets are so icy I have to go much slower than I want. It's frustrating because I need to see Nic. We've been apart a little over eight hours. That's all. And yet it feels like eight years.

Even with snow tires, the roads are difficult to navigate.

Once I arrive at my condo, I get my mail and realize I have bills due. I have to take time to pay them.

Finally, by the time I pack some clothes and other necessities over a precious hour has passed since I got off work.

I text Nic.

*I'm on my way. The roads are icy. I have to go slow.*

*I can come get you,* Nic replies.

Of course he would offer. But it's just as dangerous for him to be out there tonight.

*I'll be fine. Keep the fire going for me.*

Only after I send that last text do I realize the double-entendre. I laugh at myself.

When I drive up to Nic's cabin, everything is stark against the starlit sky. The cabin looks black outlined and tiny white lights on the background of the night and the white snow. The windows are a cherry gold, the plaid curtains open to toss light upon the icy ground.

I get out and grab my pack and my bag.

Nic opens the door and stands on the front porch with his firm arms crossed over his chest, his broad shoulders nearly blocking out all the light from the doorway.

I rush up the steps, trying not to slip, drop my bags and throw my arms around him.

He grabs me up until my feet lift off the floorboards. We're kissing like mad.

I haven't had a reception like this in, well, forever. I've been on my own for so long, I don't remember what it's like to be greeted in such an enthusiastic manner. My parents were always grumpy and tired. My boss is critical at best. This—this is something else. Something new for me.

Nic's lips are hot against mine. He's wearing only a thin shirt and black pants. No coat, but he is like a heater against me. I can feel it through my thick parka.

When he finally sets me back on my feet, he grabs my bags and leads me inside. The familiar living room and fire surround me with a cozy welcome. Nic helps me out of my coat and scarf and cap.

I smell something fantastic and look toward the kitchen. He's set up a table by the counter and on it is a feast. Mashed potatoes with melting butter, green beans, a basket of still-steaming rolls, a large wooden bowl of tossed salad, and something that looks like a pie. I think it's a cheese quiche.

I don't mind his vegetarian ways. In fact, I want to adopt them myself no matter what happens between us in a week. No matter if I never see him again.

I can't decide which I'm more hungry for at this moment, food or Nic, because I have barely eaten in the past ten hours. I figure I get to have both, but maybe not in the order I wish.

We sit and I am a hog. I eat everything I put on my plate, including all the carbs, and then help myself to seconds.

Afterwards, I sit and loll a bit in my chair, letting the food high glaze me over. I rub my tummy to aid in my digestion. I have a big grin on my face I can't control.

Nic says, "Would you like to put your stuff in the bedroom?"

Anything to get us there faster, I think.

I unpack my few clothes into a drawer Nic appoints me and hang the rest in his closet. His closet is expectedly sparse. He has a couple of suits and a couple of nice shirts, two jackets, and two pairs of pants. One is blue jeans. He does wear sweaters, too, so they must be folded inside a drawer somewhere.

With our clothes hanging side by side, nearly touching, it seems another connection is made.

Nic has a five o'clock shadow—though it's nearly three a.m. I want to touch that prickly cheek, feel his chin scrape along the skin of my inner thighs, rasp against my balls and the base of my cock.

I stand before him in the shadows of his bedroom, hands on my hips.

"Now what, Daddy?"

He steps forward, his arms coming up, his broad shoulders flexing beneath his tight, red shirt, the sleeves pulling as his biceps flex. His dark blue eyes deepen until I almost feel I'm spinning in their depths. I have no control with this man.

His hands fall to my waist. I think he's going to start with my sweater, pull it off me, but instead he begins to unbutton my pants.

"Boots first?" I make my voice small and cute.

Nic ignores my question. He pushes my pants down to my thighs. I bring one hand up to my mouth to muffle my laugh.

"What are you wearing?"

"Do you like them?"

Nic stares at my underwear, one of the items I went back to my condo to grab. They are bikini underwear, for one thing. And pink. Light baby pink with lace around the waist and thighs. My cock bulges at the crotch of the panties, pushing the elastic away from my skin and letting the tip peek out just below my belly button.

I love the way the satiny texture feels against my skin. I used a depilatory down there before work, when I was in the shower and Nic was in the other room. He doesn't know. But I found the bottle in the bathroom, figuring he had it for himself, so why shouldn't I use it as well? In the two days we were together, we were too busy for such extras. But I had been wanting to do this.

"Oh, sweet baby boy," Nic breathes.

My whole body aches to have him look at me with that expression of wonder and awe on his face. His hair shadows his forehead in shining golds and browns

Nic's hand trails along my waist until his fingers bump against the bunched lace at the waistband. His hand goes over my hip and clasps my left buttock. A smooth ride.

My pants drop to my ankles. I need to get them off, but Nic makes no move to do so. Instead, he surprises me by quickly picking me up, my pants around my ankles, and throwing me over his shoulder. When he plops me onto the center of the bed, I bounce once, then lean back and jut my hips up, giving him a great view.

My legs are bound. Nic does nothing to help me get loose; instead, he runs his hands up my shins, over my knees and to my thighs. He caresses my inner thighs and my knees bend and part, my feet still tangled in pants and boots.

He leans down and licks my belly from the lace to my hip.

My cock twitches in its own confinement. Everything feels confined even though my hands are loose. I'm still in my sweater. I'm still mostly clothed, in fact, except for my waist and my legs.

My sweater rides up, but not far. Only enough to expose my belly button and the start of my ribs.

I kick a little.

"Fussy, baby," Nic whispers, licking at my stomach again. Kissing.

I can feel the wetness on the satin of the underwear. I am thrusting upward as a small keening sound escapes my lips.

Nic presses his hand firmly on one hip to hold me still. He likes me still when he's assessing me, focusing on me, examining me.

"If I pull these down," Nic says, his face only inches from my crotch, "what might happen?"

"There's a beast in there, Daddy. A very naughty beast."

"Oh?"

"Yessss!"

Very softly, his palm runs over the bulge, snicking against the satin. The warmth of it is fast, culminating at my balls, then vanishing.

"Oh, touch me, please," I beg.

"We'll see." Nic loves this game. We've done this script in so many ways in such a short time. "Maybe you need this constriction to keep you in line. This satin cage. This cock interment."

The underwear is very tight against me. I love it but I want free now. I am throbbing at his words.

"I need you, Daddy."

"Let's just take a peek and see how bad it really is."

Oh Nic. Never one to rush things.

Nic grasps the elastic waistband and pulls it away from my skin. I feel the pressure on my cock lessen. It is freer to bob upward a bit. I look down and see Nic looking at the space where the underwear is lifted up, looking inside as if it is a surprise package containing a favorite wish.

He is so close I can feel his breath on the wet head of my cock.

"It's all right, baby. You're just fine."

"No, it needs to come off now, Daddy."

"No, I think you're all right," he says.

"But it's so stiff in there," I retort.

"Don't argue with Daddy. Daddy knows best." He holds the elastic further out, stretching it a little bit down. "See?"

My cock shivers as it meets the air, the wet tip hot and cool at the same time.

Nic says, "Perfect, just perfect. Only a little wet."

Then, I watch as his tongue comes out of his mouth and scoops up the precum dripping from the tip.

It's the lightest of touches, and so hot. I jerk my knees as Nic leans back and lets go of the waistband. It snaps back to my skin, catching the head of my cock in its tightness.

I grunt out a sound of exquisite pleasure and frustration combined. The head of my cock tingles and keeps tingling just from that one swipe of Nic's tongue.

Nic begins to take off his shirt. Watching him undress is amazing. All the golden skin begins to reveal itself, the muscles taut and stretching, his body hard in all the right places, strong and tapered, curved at certain junctures, sharp at others.

My cock drips more despite the hard hold of the elastic underwear pushing at the base of the head.

I'm breathing hard now. Pants down around my ankles, sweater pulled up over my stomach, and just watching him.

He neatly folds his shirt as he did the first night we were together, giving me a good look at his broad back which is all smooth skin and shoulder blades moving back and forth as if he had wings once, as if he could just take off and fly right around the room, touching the ceiling with his hands.

He turns and bends, giving me more good views of his arms and shoulders as he removes his boots. Then he stands and slowly undoes the buttons of his pants.

First the hip bones are revealed, and the indentations there as he slides the cloth away from his skin. He takes everything down at

74

once, underwear as well, turning to give me a side view of his backside as he bends to push the garments over his muscular thighs.

His ass is a thing to behold, round, pert, hard as a rock. I love to run my hands over it, and clutch hard as he is facing me while he fucks me, my feet in the air.

When Nic is fully naked, he turns to me. Now I can see his cock sticking out from his body, thick and long, the weight dragging it from pointing straight up. Instead, it's pointed at me.

He walks toward me, the appendage bobbing, and my mouth automatically opens.

"Baby boy, look what you've done to me." He climbs onto the bed kneeling beside me. His cock is pointing at my face, but still inches away. I lift my arms. He pushes them down. Then he says, "This is what makes you so naughty, how you behave, because then this happens." And he pushes down, rubbing his cock between my pecs. "And this." He pushes it until the dampness at the head leaves a trail down, down to my abdomen.

At that point, he lifts one leg and climbs over me. Now he straddles my waist.

"Daddy, I'm sorry. I can't help it."

"And this, look at this." He takes his cock in hand and thrusts forward until it almost touches my chin. "Your fault."

He tsks at me and shakes his head. He's so beautiful, not mean at all like some guys who try to play out something similar, or the guys in porn who are all hard and jaded and bored but do it anyway for pay.

"Daddy, what can I do? How do I make it right?"

"You probably need to be punished again. Do you think?"

I lower my eyelids. "Probably. But I forget afterward. I need to be reminded."

"Oh, I'll remind you." Nic rubs the damp tip of his cock against my chin. Then he lifts up a little on his knees, takes his hard cock in his hand and says, "Open your mouth, sweetheart. Open it wide. You need to do this for Daddy, now, because you don't know how to hold back. You need to take it now, sweetie, so you will learn."

I open my mouth and stick my tongue out a little way. The tip of Nic's cock touches just there, on the tip of my tongue, and he holds it that way for a few seconds. I taste the tart sweetness of him as if he is melting right onto my tongue. Then I tense my tongue and move it over him and around the head in circles.

"Oh, that's terrible, baby boy. That's very naughty."

I nod. "I know but I have to do it, right? It's my fault. I started this and I have to do this now to end it."

"Yes, that's a good boy who knows what is needed."

Nic thrusts lightly so his cock presses against my lips and tongue and goes partway into my mouth. I close my lips around it and begin to suck.

This is closeness and intimacy to me. This moment. All our moments, actually, but this feels so right, to give him such pleasure like this while I am all tied up in knots, my ankles bound, my cock trapped by a piece of elastic and lace.

All my feelings seem to reach out at once. I can't hold still. I can't keep my arms down. I reach up and grasp Nic's hips, my hands sliding back to his ass, and grip him hard, pulling him closer.

His cock goes deeper into my mouth and I swallow and suck, swallow and suck, my eyes wide open as I watch him throw back his head and let out a strangled cry.

His length pushes and pulls, in and out of my mouth, my tongue running over all the ridges and veins, licking everywhere I can get it to go. His balls slap my chin. Soft swollen skin. Big tight sac. He's so beautiful to me, every part of him, every inch.

I meet his gentle thrusts with little jerking bobs of my head. I feel the juices of him begin to flow, and press all the right places with my tongue, sucking hard.

Nic comes within minutes. He doesn't hold back. He lets me take him like that and bring him this rushed orgasm as if he, too, has been waiting all night for my return. Ten short hours apart, and it's come to this.

Spurts of pleasure fill my mouth. I swallow it all, sucking that throbbing cock through to the finish. When he pulls out, I unclasp my hands from his ass and wipe my mouth.

"Good boy." Nic's smile turns to a white, toothy grin. He moves until he's kneeling at my side again, and glances at my middle, his gaze warm and hazy, half-lidded.

"That little boy cock of yours is very stiff." That's all he says.

I nod and gulp, still tasting him, still wanting more of him. I'd suck his cock all night if he'd let me.

He leans toward my bulge. Again I feel his breath. I am trapped and yet happy. So happy. Whatever he does or wants to do, I am more content than ever.

I look down my body and I can see my cockhead pushing out beyond the elastic of the underwear. The pale, sweet baby pink underwear. With lace at the thighs and the top. With little embroidered tulips on the left side. I wonder if Nic had noticed them, or if he's seeing them now. They are pink, too, and blend in so they are subtle. Sort of like a secret.

There are, I think, so many secrets here. Waiting to be revealed.

Nic puts his hand on my balls, and squeezes through the satin material. As he does, the tip of my cock dribbles, wetting that area of my stomach.

I look at him bent over me, his ass so hard and round, his cock still jutting hard from his middle. He tongues the head of my cock again, where it pushes past the elastic.

"Oh, Daddy!"

It tingles and my balls feel like they're moving all over the place in their pouch.

"Turn over now, baby boy," Nic instructs, sitting up again. Much to my disappointment.

I obey immediately, getting my knees under me though my ankles are bound. Using my hands to balance. Should I lie flat or with my knees under me? I wait for instruction.

"That's a good boy."

Nic grabs the back of the underwear and pulls them over my ass, revealing it. "Knees underneath you now, sweetheart," Nic says.

I pull them up to my chest and stick my ass in the air.

"Good boy." He pats my lower back, then caresses the globes of my ass until my skin is raging all over as if on fire. He parts the cheeks and I can feel his breath down there, all hot and curious. Then that sensation leaves me and I crane my neck to look around my shoulder.

"You—you freshly shaved yourself?" Nic asks.

Oh. That. "Yes, Daddy. I thought it would be best. Cleaner. I keep myself trimmed but the hair was growing back. Did I do right, Daddy?"

"Oh, yes, you did right, baby. You thought that through very well."

I love the praise. "Thank you, Daddy."

"It's perfect. Now I can really see that sweet little pink bud of yours like a flower just waiting to bloom."

He touches me there. I gasp. Then I feel his tongue and I am lost in a haze of white immensity that embraces me, drapes me in great love and caring like I've never known.

Nic licks me and, with his tongue and one finger, opens me up. I feel the intrusion, finger and wet muscle, like warm loving, like whole new worlds are being formed from just that touch.

I'm not exaggerating. This guy has me under his thumb, and more. I'm completely overtaken. Broken up into a thousand little pieces and gently put back together again.

Finally, when it seems I can take no more, I'm going to come whether he touches my cock or not, he pulls away.

"Turn over, baby."

I comply, getting onto my back again.

"Raise your knees up as high as you can."

I still have my pants around my ankles, and my boots on. I lift my legs. Nic puts a hand underneath me and helps me.

"You can bend your knees, boy," he says.

I bend my knees and Nic helps me push them until they nearly touch my chest. My boot-clad feet are in the air above me. My butt is bent and exposed. The underwear still covers my cock—well, most of it. But as I bend that way, my balls drop out from their satin cage.

Nic says, "You freshly shaved all over? Including around your balls and cock?"

"Yes, Daddy."

"Hmm. Just a minute. Lower your legs again."

I let my feet down, my knees still bent. Nic grabs the waistband and pulls it down so that it constricts my thighs. My cock finally waves free, slapping my stomach.

Nic then touches the naked base and runs his hands down over my balls.

He leans in. "You are completely hairless now, sweet boy. What got into you?"

"I just thought it would make me better, Daddy. Cleaner."

"Yes, baby. Yes, it does."

So he likes it. Every part of me is naked now, hairless, and the air touching my skin makes me even more sensitive.

Nic pulls the underwear all the way down my legs to my ankles where it bunches pinkly with my pants.

"Let's get your legs up again, sweetie," Nic says.

I know what to do this time, but his hands help me support the weight of pulling my bent knees to my chest, my boots in the air.

Nic has lube in his hand which I never saw him grab. He eases his fingers into my hole. But I'm already bloomed, already open for him.

He doesn't have to do much more than oil his own length, which has never gone down even though I gave him a very thorough blowjob.

He lines himself up and eases into me. I am ready. I am so ready. His cock slides neatly, slowly, filling me up, and I feel no pain. I'm too aroused for that. Already too overly sensitized to anything but pleasure and more pleasure.

Nic fucks me like that until I'm crying out. When I make that sound, he pulls out, and I whimper.

"Turn over, baby," he orders.

I turn again. On my back, on my knees, however many times he wants to change position, I'm ready. I want it. Any way I can get it.

Now I am on my knees.

He does not plunge right back into me. Instead, he touches my hole and says, "It's so open. Wide and waiting and wanting. Just how I love my boy."

"Yes, Daddy." I wiggle my ass.

He plays with my balls, then he milks my cock. It feels so good.

He licks at my balls, and as he does so, pulls my cock straight down and milks downward, toward the mattress.

"Oh, yes!" I can't help but encourage more.

He leans further between my legs, his scruff rough against my balls, and angles my cock backward toward his mouth, taking the tip between his lips, tonguing it, then sucking.

I can't come like that. At that angle. It's infuriating.

He sucks me until I nearly scream, then lets me go and milks downward again, this time tight and fast and I scream.

The orgasm rolls through me, and my cock throbs and sprays the bedcovers. Daddy will have to wash them yet again. I'm not sorry.

With his hand still on my cock, rubbing me through my orgasm, Nic plunges into me again. He fucks me fast and hard now, milking my cock downward, until only a couple minutes pass and another orgasm erupts from me. As if the first wasn't enough, blasting through me like no tomorrow. This one is slow and takes me high, high up, and rumbles through me. My cock shoots hard a couple times, then continues to drip as my muscles spasm.

Nic says, "Oh baby, that's so sweet. You're so tight. That grip, oh!"

Whatever I'm doing affects him, and I feel the warm liquid fill me up as he comes for his second time as well.

After that, I barely feel him pull out as I start to nod off. But I'm not too far gone to feel him undo my boots, pull them off one by one, and take away my pants and underwear. He lets me keep my sweater, so I'm naked from the waist down, then he gets into the bed and curls up at my back, pulling me tightly to him.

I bend my knees. I press back, and fall instantly to sleep.

# Chapter Eight

## Nic

"Wait up for me?" Angelbaby tosses a look over his shoulder as he walks onto the porch. He's leaving me for another eight to ten hours. Work.

"Of course. Always."

In the days we've spent together in this steamy, glittery cabin, Angel and I have synched our routines. I'm practically nocturnal now, which is great leading up to Christmas, because I do that gig, even with the help of time-slips, in one frantic twenty-four hour period.

He talks about taking days off work, but I don't want him to miss any. I don't want his paychecks to dwindle because when I'm gone, he'll still need money and a job.

We can work around his job. And it gives him his world back for a little while, as well, since I fully realize I can be a bit overwhelming in my desires and demands. Not that Angel seems to mind.

Every day he leaves, I plan a late-late dinner to greet him with. I love to bake. I don't use my magic for that, like I do magic for decorating. Cooking is fun. Baking. Even more fun. Maybe it's because I love sweets. Elves, reindeer, myself—we live mostly on sweets. We eat other good things as well, but sweets are the staple food in Santa's Village and the hidden City of the North.

Angel. *Angelbaby.* Sometimes all I need to do is think of him and my eyes fill, the sting against the lids both good and bad. He's not worn out his welcome, that is a sure thing.

I find myself walking about the cabin while he is gone gripping the air with my fingers, as if I can feel his skin and muscle and hair against me, in my arms, in my hands. I want him always touching me, but that can't work, of course. It's impossible. People need breathing room. Freedom.

He is so perfect in every way. As a human being. As a man. And as the boy to my daddy persona, my need to care and give and dominate and possess. He has never once complained—unless I make him wait too long for satisfaction. But even then, he enjoys my techniques, my bedroom preferences. Always eager to do as I wish, to obey. And the way he clings to me.

I give a little sniff. I will miss that when I am gone from here.

I will have to deal with that, though. He has a life here, not a part of elfland or magic. He should be allowed to live it.

I hope I'm not making a mistake. I hope I'm doing the right thing here, letting Angel go, letting him find his way. He will have a good life, I can already sense it inside him, the way I sense whether people are good or bad. The way I can read people's soul-cores, and see if they are matched or mismatched, trapped or free, happy or sad.

Angel is not truly a naughty boy in the outside sense of that word. He's young and has yet to grow, to mature. He wants nice things, which is not a crime. He wants contentment. He will explore the world and find it; I know this in my heart.

But the way he hugs me in his sleep. The way he smiles. How his skin flushes as I caress him, spank him, make love to him. The way he kisses and holds onto me as we greet, as we part—each day. How his wild hair is swept up by starlight. The way his eyes turn to slits as I sate him. The way he has an ability at such a young age to hold a real conversation without dissolving into giggles.

Yes I love the boy inside him, but I love the intellect, too. I have treasure here right now in the palms of my hands. I have real wealth. I don't want to let it fall like melting snow through my fingers.

But I have to. I have to because I have a job, and he has a job. Because I am elfin and he is human. Because this is how it works. Our two worlds mesh very little. Our two worlds live side by side but we, my elves, reindeer and I, are the unknown entity.

I go about my puttering all day, realizing the fragile world we have created with each other is, like spun sugar, about to dissolve under the pressure of the time we have left.

I leave in two days.

Two days is not long enough. It's barely enough time to explore his body all the many more times I need. A thousand times would not be enough. A million.

I have no one to talk to about this. My servant, Wist, who has been with me for almost two hundred years, is dear to me, but not technically my friend. We do not confide in each other.

82

He has been married twice. He has had a family as well. He is lovely, and he is loyal, but—no, we do not talk of such things as relationships, love, sex.

It's only nine p.m., but I am restless for Angel. Any thoughts I have of going back to Prancer's and being around him while he works I've managed to stuff away, deny.

But tonight I want to see him. Something draws me. And I am thirsty.

It's probably a big mistake.

But I find myself turning into the parking lot of Prancer's in my rented Chevy Camaro.

The lot has been salted and treated with brine and sand so the cars don't get stuck or slide into each other from the icy conditions. I park next to a big purple Jeep on one side, and a dark blue Dodge Ram pickup on the other.

That's Alaska for you. Most people out here where the towns are small and the woods are deep drive big work vehicles. They don't just want them, they need them. They don't have sleighs to get them around in the wintertime. They don't have flying reindeer.

I get out of my car and step onto the cleared asphalt.

The lights from Prancer's bleed out through the glass doors as they open and close. The windows are darkened, but still illuminated from within to a shade of blue. A reindeer bounding over a crescent moon illuminates a sign on the lightly snow-covered porch roof over the door. The word Prancer's is lit up and flashing neon pink.

The place could have been a dive, but it's rather nice, which was why I'd stopped by for a drink in the first place. I had walked the roads one night, needing to move through unknown territory. To exercise my muscles. To think. To be myself far away from my known territory and my role as Santa in Santa's Village.

I never would have found the place if I hadn't gone out. The walk had taken over two hours. And then two hours home, thinking of Angelbaby all the way through the coldest part of the November night.

The cold did not affect me, but I was aware of it. The sharp edge of the air, the scent of frozen pinesap, the crispness of icy mist making clouds before me with every breath I exhaled. And that pretty, pretty boy on my mind with every step that took me further away from him.

I had not known after I left him my number if he would even call. Waiters at places like Prancer's get solicited right and left, I'm sure. Angel could have ignored it. And me. But he didn't.

It was as if that night I walked the dark and curving roads specifically to find him. To find my fate.

But I did not allow myself to think like that. I had never brought a human to my real home, and I hadn't planned to start.

Now, here I am walking up the steps of Prancer's because I cannot stay away from one human. A possessive surge runs through my veins as I open the door to the entryway, stomp my boots to make sure the ice comes off, then open the second door to peer inside the bar teeming with male patrons of all ages, hues and sizes.

As I remove my jacket and scarf, I cannot help but scan the entire establishment and all the clusters of humans to locate Angel. It turns out to be easy enough. For he stands out. He glows. The colors of him sparkle to my vision: light blue, pale gold, and pinks that tinge the edges of his beauty, his aura.

His lean frame seems to rise up from his black leather trousers like a sculpture, the muscles of his arms flexing as he carries a tray laden with drinks to a noisy round table at the back near the kitchen door.

He is the most beautiful human in the entire place with his long legs and his graceful walk even as he carries the weight of his tray. His blond hair tumbles behind him, just short of shoulder length, sprayed and glistening gold to match the glitter on his hairless chest and arms.

He is unique and I cannot help but think of him as mine even though in just two days, I am going to have to give him up. My heart skips a beat at the thought.

I walk up to the bar and take a seat between two guys who couldn't be more different from each other. One sports a bushy beard and wears camouflage cargo pants and a thick black pullover. The other has pink hair and a black net shirt that shows off his nipple and navel piercings. His skinny black jeans are slit at the sides from thigh to ankle and held together with links of shiny silver chain.

A bartender tosses a coaster with the Prancer's logo on it. It lands on the shining counter in front of me as he asks for my order.

"Rum and Coke." I want alcohol, but I also want the sugar.

He immediately makes my order and sets it in front of me.

I hear the shouts and drunken laughter of the noisy table where Angel is delivering drinks. I flinch and feel a strange heat go through me as I watch one of the customers assault my boy by running his hand over the tight black leather-clad curve of his ass.

Ignoring my drink, I start to stand, oblivious to the rest of the crowd around me, attention focused solely on Angel. As I watch, my fists clenched, Angel handles himself with quite a performance. He gives a little whirl until he's out of arm's reach of the assaulter, and I see him grin as he shakes his head and crooks his forefinger at the guy's face.

The guy takes it in stride, like a joke, and hands Angel a crisp bill. Hopefully that tip is a high denomination. Angel doesn't deserve any less.

I watch how he owns that table, how his charisma gets more orders and more tips. Still, I am livid. Men pawing my baby boy? This can't be right.

Slowly, I take my seat again, but keep my body turned away from the bar. I can't take my eyes off Angel. I ignore my drink.

As if sensing something, Angel turns from the busy table and swivels his blond head to look right at me. His eyebrows rise. His mouth opens in surprise. He smiles and waves.

I wave back.

This world is beautiful. I won't argue it. But this world can be gaudy and torrid as well. And my boy –for I do think of him as mine now—at twenty-two years old is in it all on his own. His parents were never there for him. He has no siblings he's ever spoken of. He's gay and he's beautiful and he spins through the crowd like they're his garden. He's pulling at the weeds and taking the blooms. Some day he will make a bouquet of all he has wrought.

I am not one of them. I am separate. Another species altogether. Immortal. I cannot offer him the life he's accustomed to here. I cannot be the lone tree in this garden, the one that remains frozen and gives little shade. The one that never changes with the seasons, never dies. I have to live away from humans for the most part because of that.

My elves are the same way. They are not immortal, but they are long-lived. And they have points on their ears that might make them stand out in a crowd.

I don't have pointy ears, but I still have enough differences and abilities that must remain secret, thus I allow myself only short ventures into the human realm.

All this rushes through my mind in a flash, like a light bulb going off. The reasons I must leave. The reasons I cannot keep Angel all for myself.

It does not mean, as I watch Angel move through the crowd, lithe and bright, graceful and lively, that I don't have regrets. For myself, a lonely fool for pretty boys who love to be dominated and coddled. And for Angel who cannot hide his impending sadness in my presence as the days grow closer to my departure.

If only I had never stopped in at Prancer's that night of my lonely, dark walk through the cold. If only I had continued by, not drawn by a cartoon image of a flying reindeer, or the knowledge that this place was a gay bar which catered to my very core self.

I would never have met Angel.

But to never have met him—to think that it might have been better all the way around for me and for him—seems a crime against what we have shared. What we have.

The connection between us feels sacred. I'm a beast for even thinking it should not exist. These past days have been all good, a divine experience, a coming together of two lonely souls who, like puzzle pieces, fit together by design.

I believe in fate. I believe we make our own fate. Both can be true at the same time. Angel and I have made this time together into a beautiful experience. As if it were meant to be.

I do not belittle that. I honor it.

It will be hard to leave him, yes, but this time in my life has been incredible and everything I needed to re-energize me.

I watch Angel set his tray on the end of the bar and come around to greet me, hands free. I turn on the stool. He walks right up to me and puts his arms around my neck, pulling me into a sweet kiss. Right in front of the patrons. In front of his boss and co-workers. In front of everyone.

My face heats but I kiss him back with my hand ruffling the stiffness of his sprayed back hair.

"Nic, I didn't know you'd be dropping by."

"I almost didn't. I've held back because I don't want to interfere with your work."

86

"Interfere?" He steps back, arms criss crossing over his chest. "You are anything but an interference. This is where we met!"

"Yes."

"The symbol of us is, in my mind, a silly flying reindeer."

Silly indeed. It is the symbol of my heart of hearts. My reindeer are like my children, loyal and loving. I love them more than life itself.

As usual, Angel hits me to the core with his words, not knowing the truth, though somewhere in his subconscious he senses it. Knowing without knowing, as humans tend to do when faced with the unknown. He feels me on deeper levels he's barely begun to try and figure out.

"I'm glad you came by, Nic. Really, I am."

"I'm glad, too."

Then, with an expression of sudden horror, he asks, "You didn't walk, did you?"

"No, I drove."

He nods. "I'm so happy you're here." His brown eyes brim with a sheen that catches all the light in the room. He looks like he wants to say more, but isn't sure what that might be.

"I missed you, too," I say.

His grin turns to a shy smile and he ducks his head, his cheeks tinged pink. "Now I surely won't be able to concentrate for the rest of my shift."

I chuckle. He makes it so easy for me to laugh with him. But that ease comes with pain. I want to hold him to me. I want to keep him. Confine him. Never let him go.

What terrible thoughts. I *am* a beast! An alien intruder into a world of human inhabitants. It's their world, not mine. I have no right to think these thoughts of taking Angel away from all of this.

And confinement? I have my kinks, but that is the last straw. I would never want to hinder Angel's freedom, his beautiful essence which is meant to grow and evolve through his own being, his authentic self.

I know these things. I've lived a long time. One does not try to mold, confine or trap another being. It's wrong. I don't even eat animals, for heaven's sake.

A table of partiers waves to get Angel's attention.

"I'll be right back," he says, then gives a little hop and rushes to assist them with drink or appetizer orders.

Two more days until I leave.

I want to be in Angel's presence the entire time. I don't want to waste a moment. That's why I have come here tonight, I decide. That's what drew me here. Not the watered-down booze. Not the crowd. Just Angel. My Angelbaby.

When did I start thinking of him as *mine*? From the minute I met him. And I will go back to my village and continue the thought no matter how many years pass, no matter if my heart breaks and renews itself in other ways. Angelbaby will always be mine.

When Angel gets a break, he motions me to follow him to a small back room for staff only. There are three round tables back there, and a few old, rough-looking chairs.

We sit and eat chili-fries together. He gets the chili on the side so I don't have to touch the meat. We eat and mostly stare into each other's eyes.

"I'm so glad you came tonight. I've been thinking."

"About what?" I ask.

"You leave soon, right?"

My throat closes a little. I nod.

"I have Tuesday off again. That's tomorrow. The bar is closed. But I'll take Wednesday off, too. We'll have that whole time together, no interruptions."

Angel looks down as his eyes glimmer. He reaches across the unpolished wood of the table, his fingernails rubbing the unvarnished wood, and places his hand on top of mine.

I turn my hand over and grasp his. I don't want to let him go. I can't say it in words, though. I can't.

"It sounds like a good plan." I manage to force a calm simplicity to my tone.

Angel's naked, glittery chest rises and falls. I wish we were in my cabin right now. I wish I could take him into my arms and hold him tight, feel his breathing and his heartbeat close to my skin as if we are one single thrum of life joined together with two souls in tandem. Ever circling.

After Angel's break, I stay at Prancer's until is shift his over. I slowly drink a couple more rum and Cokes. They have little effect on me except to make me relax. And crave more sugar.

I tip the bartender nicely, and he brings me a free plate of nachos, no meat. Angel must have tipped him off on my vegetarian status.

When Angel is changed and in his parka, scarf and hat, I follow him outside to the cold and icy parking lot. He drives behind me all the way home to my cabin.

Once inside, he throws himself on me, his arms and legs circling me, and I hold him up off the ground and hug him tight until he is gasping.

After we make love, I stay awake for a long while watching him sleep, tousled and naked in my arms. I draw the covers over us, tucking him in. I enclose him in an embrace that is possessive, but is also about forming a body memory, a muscle memory. I want to retain the feel of him pressed against me in my mind forever.

I hold him to me. I wrap my arms and legs tighter around him until it feels like maybe I am hurting him. He shifts and his eyelids flutter, but he never makes a sound of protest, not a peep, not my good baby boy, not my sweetheart, my love. Yes, my love.

# Chapter Nine

## Angel

"I want you to tell me something about yourself you've never told me. Something you don't tell most people, or anyone at all," I say.

We're sitting on the couch, me and Nic, the fire flaring up in tarnish and rust, the TV softly playing *Wedding Crashers* which I have seen nine times, and Nic has seen twice.

I'm in Nic's lap, leaning back against his chest. We're both naked, but we have a big blanket covering us, up to my waist. I can feel the planes and cords of his muscles pressing me. His thighs, rock hard, are almost bruising to sit on, and he senses this, letting them spread so my butt falls down to the cushion. His half hard cock presses the side of my hip.

"Such as?" he asks.

He has delay tactics he employs when talking about himself. He always answers my questions with questions of his own. It is infuriating. And delightful.

"Such as something you don't often tell people. Like a secret. Like you have a secret love child stashed in a foreign country at a boarding school and no one knows, not even the child, who thinks he is your ward."

"Is that the plot of the next movie we're going to watch?" Nic asks.

I chuckle. "Or you have a wife and she's super creepy and out of her mind and you keep her locked in an attic and only your most devoted and loyal servant knows about her and brings her food twice a day."

Nic sighs and wraps both arms around my chest. "I will tell you something if you tell me something."

"Deal."

Really, I know so little about him. He behaves as if his job is uninteresting, something I might find boring. And he never says exactly where it is he lives when he's not on vacation in Alaska and renting a cabin elaborately decorated for the holidays he won't be here to enjoy.

Silence.

"Okay, I'll go first," I say.

It's hard to think. I scrunch up my face. I put a hand to my forehead.

There are several things in my life I don't talk to others about. Confiding in people is hard for me. Of course I have friends, and had friends growing up, but I never felt as close to them as I wanted or hoped. It has been difficult for me to form lasting relationships. My parents never instilled it in me. Or maybe I was born weird that way.

Some things I don't feel comfortable talking about with anyone.

"Okay, I have one. Something I don't tell people because it's just weird and sort of negative and might make them define me a certain way."

"What?" Nic says, his hands moving up and down my chest. "You're gay?"

"Hah. So funny." I take a deep breath. "I had leukemia when I was four years old. I remember every detail. I was in the hospital for two weeks and I heard the doctors tell my parents I would not make it. My mom cried. My dad patted my head. They left me every day and still went to work. They had jobs they could not afford to lose.

"I lay in the hospital bed alone and scared and feeling really small among all the lights and machines and the white white sheets and the strangers—nurses—coming in to see me and poke me and prod me all the time. I was so scared.

"One day a man came. He had on this weird white shirt. I remember it was pleated at the throat and had no buttons or zippers, but was really tight at his neck. He had really long fingers and I remember him talking to me but I can't really remember everything he said. He was sort of old—well, everyone is old when you're four. He had no hair on his head and the lights of the monitors reflected on his scalp. His eyes were pale blue.

"He talked to me for a long time. I remember him saying one thing just before he left. He said, *Always remember who you are and you won't steer wrong during the storms.*

"It is so weird. I remember those words, but I don't remember the context. I thought I dreamed him. For years I convinced myself it was a dream.

"But later the doctors returned with new tests that said I was better. I guess I went into remission? I never asked. My parents didn't talk about it. But I didn't die. And so, here I am."

I grin up at Nic's face.

He looks a bit shocked. "That's—that's fascinating," he says.

"Yeah, but weird. You don't think I'm too weird that I remember that, right? It was probably a dream but it didn't feel like it."

"No. Not at all. You're not weird. That's a wonderful story. Quite amazing." He hugs me tight.

"Yeah, there's a lot of stuff maybe we can't always explain but it just happens to us. To some people. Maybe to everyone. But people don't talk about stuff like that. You know, like UFOs and shit. I don't. But I'm glad I told you. It's one of my secrets and, well, now I've given it to you."

"Thank you for trusting me enough to tell me," Nic says. He kisses my forehead.

I shut my eyes and try not to think about the fact that after one more night I won't have him anymore. He won't be here. He'll vanish like smoke. Like mist. As if he never was. Like the guy who visited me in the hospital. But I'll remember. I'll always remember.

Nic's voice is low and private as he speaks. "All right. I'll tell you something about myself."

He takes a deep breath. "My grandmother raised me and taught me. She was very old. Ancient. Always ancient to my child point of view. You know, ageless. But fascinating. Powerful. She was what people called a sorcerer, or witch.

"I learned some of her same techniques."

"You mean you're a witch?"

"In a manner of speaking. At least, the way you might think. I don't call myself that, though."

"That's awesome. But, like, what do you do? Read minds and stuff?"

Nic bows his head. "And stuff."

I want to say that maybe someday he'll show me. But I clamp down on the words. There is no someday with us. There is only now. Unless Nic changes his mind.

I keep wracking my brain trying to think of a way to entice him to stay. But that sort of thinking isn't fair to him. I may be a bit of a brat and love my luxury, but I'm not manipulative in that way. Not in matters of the heart. Not when it is about a person's life.

"Nic. I—I mean Daddy. I feel so close to you right now." I bury my head in his hard, flat chest.

*

We are bordering on darkness, the road up ahead coming to an end. Our last night.

I can see it clearer and clearer—the ending of us—but I don't want to. I'll be forced to disembark from this place I've loved so much, and leave behind our lovely routine filled with ecstasy and joy.

My throat feels all closed up today. My chest quivers with a ghostly ache. My eyes are big and always feel filled up with moisture ready to let go if I move wrong, or if Nic looks at me too intently.

I can't meet his eyes as I eat. We made love in the morning and I hid my face against his shoulder the entire time. I can barely abide his touch anymore, not because I hate it but because I love it too much. Too much to let it go. I can't imagine never having this again.

I suppose he might return next year, or any time actually, but am I to be only his lover when he comes to port? When he comes ashore from his northern, mysterious activities?

I don't think I can handle that. I want any scrap he'll give me, I tell myself. But if it hurts too much, well, I won't handle that gracefully. I know myself too well. I'll become angry and reckless and more and more *naughty*, to use Nic's favorite word. I'll rush to fill all the holes and hollow empty voids inside me and live in a fucked up world of regret.

Nic has ruined me.

At lunch, which we have around four o'clock because we're completely off normal human schedules, I pick at my food.

Nic watches me for a while with those sea-dark eyes of his, then abruptly stands and comes around to my chair. He leans down and picks me up, cradle style, wrapping his arms around me. I'm wearing only slippers and a robe and it falls open on my thighs.

I make a deep sound in my throat, almost a cry.

Nic nuzzles me and carries me off to the rug in front of the fireplace. It's warm and cozy there. We've piled up a mountain of pillows—where did he get them all?

He kneels, placing me gently on the pillows. He leans over me, his blond hair nearly in his eyes.

"Look at me," he says softly.

I scrunch my eyes closed.

"Angelbaby. Open your eyes."

I turn my head away.

Nic says nothing. I hear him breath in and out. I hear a shushed thumping that sounds like his heart, then realize it's my own. The fire is a fever to my right. Nic is the resulting delirium to my left.

Nic's large hand presses the side of my head. His fingers weave through my hair, the tips rubbing at my scalp and giving me little all-over shivers. He pats my hair, and his hand moves down to caress my forehead and cup my cheek.

I keep my eyes shut as slowly he caresses me. Moving down with that whispery touch to my chin, my neck. He parts my robe and the warm air flows against my bare chest. His hands explore me, frame me, touch me.

I bite on the insides of my lips to keep quiet. My body thrums.

Palms and fingertips spread over my stomach and waist, as if painting me with touch, warmth, the very air between us.

My cock, which has already had much pleasure today, still has energy to rise. For him. For my daddy. It's bare, hairless still, only a shadow of stubble growing back from where I used the depilatory and shaved the leftover hair away.

Nic's hands hold me around the waist, fingers digging into my back, thumbs against my belly.

I keep my eyelids clenched, like my fists at my side. My lungs heave. Something hurts me down, down through the layers of existence, of being, of self. An ache so deep it's like a pull of gravity from inside and out, wrenching me.

I think of Nic telling me he is a sorcerer and what that might mean. In this moment, it means his touch is magic. It's everything to me, and I want to bask in this minute, this hour, but my nerves won't allow it. And that ache. That ache I can't reach to soothe the inner cramp of it threatens to control me more than my daddy, more than being happy I am lucky enough to have had these eleven days with such a man.

Hands move to caress my upper thighs, my legs, my ankles and feet.

Hands go back up. Fingers lightly caress my balls and the shaft of my cock. Strong arms turn me and now the hands explore my back, my ass, the backs of my thighs.

I sob into a pillow, face down, my arms around it hugging it to me.

I'm a broken dream. But I will have this memory always.

Nic lies down beside me and holds me to him. Tears flood my closed eyes threatening to escape, the sting of a hundred needles at once.

Nic whispers in my ear. "Oh, baby, you sweet sweet heart."

I lose it and cough to try to hide my feelings. I press my now hard cock against his abdomen. I tangle my legs with his. I force my way half on top of him, putting my arms around his neck, pulling with all my strength.

Nic rubs my back slowly, and his lips trail over my forehead.

The fire at my back, the delirium at my front.

I never open my eyes and fall into a doze, my body only relaxing when in complete contact with his.

\*

Nic puts me on the bed, face down and instructs me to lift my hips.

I disobey and keep myself flat.

I don't want to be spanked now. I feel too terrible. I want to use these last hours with Nic to be with him, to feel him, to have him consume me, but I also only want to sleep until I can forget. Forget that he's leaving. Forget that deep maddening ache spreading through my core like a disease.

"Naughty boy. On your knees," Nic says.

I gasp and remain still.

Hands caress my ass, warm and grasping.

"All right, we can do this lying down, too."

I do not move.

"Angelbaby, do you want to use your safe word *moonlight*?"

No. There are no safe words with Nic. Nothing is safe for me anymore. I don't want to say it. I want him to do whatever he wants. I don't want him to stop. Ever. That's all I ask. Nothing too grand, right? Just that he never stops.

When I do not respond, Nic slaps my right cheek and the sensation goes through me like an electric jolt. I push my face into the pillow and hold my breath.

The next smack comes to my left cheek.

I say nothing. Safety has runs its course. I'm in a place where I have no need for safe words, where nothing matters. Where any touch Nic gives me is wanted, desired, craved. Needed like my next breath.

The spanking continues. I hear Nic breathing hard through it all. I am a bad boy. I need this. I want this. I don't want this. I hate it. I love it. I am so utterly confused.

When he finishes, the world has stopped turning. I can feel it. Time stopping though the clock still runs and people still inhabit the planet and run their daily routines, worn out but still racing through each day.

But for me, this second, this minute is the single focal point in time where I am forever stopped, my heart, my brain, my lungs still work, but I am stopped. Frozen here. A boy made of snow that will never again melt even if I am thrown into the sun itself.

Nic gives a little cry and drops on top of me, his weight the only tangible thing to my mind right now.

After a while, he moves lubed fingers inside me, then his cock warm and hard. Thrusting in and out of me as his hands hold my cheeks open, as he fucks me to own me.

I want to tell him. He does own me. That's the problem. That's the big deal here. He owns me and now I am ruined for any future without him.

My cock is hard against the mattress. Unlike the deep ache inside me, it throbs with an agony of pleasure. I come fast but wordless, clenching as Nic fills me.

Nic mumbles something I cannot hear or understand because the whiteness of ecstasy has momentarily deafened me. I feel when he comes, too, though, as I'm on my way down floating in a haze of black flakes on a gray background. A heat fills my ass and my passage identifies his throb of orgasm.

A soft towel cleans me. Strong arms surround me.

Still, I say nothing. That is what I remember.

\*

I wake to a gray light that makes the air of the bedroom feel stagnant and cold. I have no idea what time it is. But I do know one thing. I can feel it to my bones. I don't have to reach across the bed to confirm.

Nic is gone.

I get up and my muscles ache all over. My ass is sore both inside and out. Usually a heady, wonderful feeling, now it is annoying.

I put on my robe and wander down the hall. I do not call his name. I do not want my voice to sting this silence and make it any worse.

The lights are still on all over the living room. The twinkling ones on the tree, and the white-gold ones that frame the mantel. The fire, however, is dead.

And all the static and charge of the air of this cabin when we were together is gone. Cold seeps in through the cracks of windows and doors, though the heat has been left on.

My throat closes. I gasp one breath, then two. I shut my eyes to feel my tears but there are none. They are dry. Like my body and my mind. Dry and listless and thirsting. As it will be forevermore.

# Chapter Ten

## Nic

Flying reindeer are very smart. They don't really need a master. I take the role because they allow it. Not because I control them. They can drive themselves. They know how to pull a sleigh with their eyes closed.

I made the plan months ago. My cabin. My retreat. My vacation away from all I am responsible for with the elves, with the City of the North, with my ice castle.

I made the plan for my eight lovely reindeer and my sleigh to meet me in these still dark woods this morning. Daylight in late November in this part of Alaska has dwindled to seven hours.

It's nine a.m. and the sun is just coming up, turning the sky lavender above the green stripe on the eastern horizon where mountains begin. West of me, a thick wood obscures all things of Man.

This tundra-like clearing is perfect for landings and take offs.

As I crunch through deep snow in my thick boots, in my red jacket and my scarf and a small back of personal items in my hand, the deer snort and stomp in the snow, their breaths steaming from their noses. They turn to look at me as I approach.

The candy apple red sleigh gleams in perfect condition. My loyal elves no doubt polished it all day yesterday in preparation for this trip.

I walk around the back of the sleigh and throw my bag inside. Then I walk past each deer and run my hands down their backs and pat their long noses. Each one is precious to me. Each magic animal has his own name and unique intelligent look in his eyes.

They paw the snow. Their eyes glow with excitement. They love to fly high up in the sky. Long distances do not faze them.

"Thank you all," I say. My voice crackles as if out of use. I clear my throat and take a deep, shuddering breath. "Will you take me home?"

They all toss their heads in answer. *Yes.*

Home is the North Pole. Santa's Village. It has nothing to do with the lie I told Angel. Lies.

I bow my head.

The deer closest to me, Donner, lifts his nose and sniffs the air. He makes a strange, strangled noise that almost sounds like speech. Almost sounds like, *Santa are you well?*

"All is well," I reply.

He sniffs again, and shakes his head.

I swallow hard, then walk to the sleigh and board her. The reins are neatly in their runnels, tied off so they don't get tangled and blow around as the reindeer travel without me at the sleigh's helm.

Before I grab the reins, I close my eyes and summon the magic. It's like warmth and starlight breathing through me, my magic, and through it I create. It is my artist's tool. I made Santa's Village by magic alone. I made the City of the North where most elves live. I made my ice castle on pure thought alone with the depths of training my grandmother taught me.

Now I create a bubble around the sleigh and the deer. Cold does not bother us, but the wind at higher elevations is relentless and can tear off harnesses, hats, coats, clothes. It would easily tear my bag from the back and send it spiraling to Earth.

Once the bubble is complete, I take the reins. I call the deer. Each by name. Each one deserving special attention. I end with my usual order.

"Dash away all!"

They begin their run and the sleigh glides effortlessly along the snow and ice. Faster and faster we go until the two lead deer, Dasher and Dancer, lift off. The rest follow and we're airborne.

My stomach tenses in pleasure. I look down. I see the woods still dark against the white of the ground, and the distant mountains where the sun is an orange crescent just beginning to peek over the fanged edges of towering terrain.

The reindeer make a wide turn curving us around and over the wood where we are least visible. I don't hit the cloak button yet. Anyone about looking up through thick foliage will see only spots of sky and if they see movement at all, they will think we are a bird.

Beyond those woods is the cabin I lived in for two weeks.

I clamp down on that thought, but it does no good. I imagine Angel waking to the empty house, searching for me but knowing I am gone. I can see his young face down-turned, his sweet brown eyes dulling over. I can still scent the glimmering summer shine of him, the exuberance of his personality, and taste his lips upon mine sweet and pure and giving.

Leaving him behind brings a deep pain not unlike two centuries ago when I had to leave my whole dying world with the elves I could gather and my magic deer and flee into the human realm.

But it is what must be. No human has ever come into the village. Or the city. No human knows of our existence. We are myth. We are legend. We are poems and stories to be told on snowy nights in front of the blaze of a hearth and the beauty of a pine clad tree in shining lights and ornaments.

We are the dream that vanishes in the light of day. We are a glimpse and a glimmer, hope topped with a child-like smile. We are December crouched at the end of a year and wishes held upon stars caught in the tops of trees.

We gather in your thoughts when the stores are closed and the hours dark like a moment of freedom from all, that point in your mind when you just let go for a few seconds of total energy, of being yourself unhindered by daily routine. We are the sparkle of the love you thought was lost returned.

Deep inside Angel, he knows this. He knows me without being able to put into words my actual identity, and understands why this separation must occur.

The big question is, do I know? Do I really understand my decision? My reasoning?

Because I don't understand. I don't feel it. And the tears on my face testify to this as fact. My laugh is gone. My jolly demeanor.

I flick my wrists and the reins ripple. The deer go higher and faster, leaving Alaska, leaving my Angelbaby behind.

\*

"How was your vacation, sir?" Wist takes my jacket, hat and scarf. He is an elder elf with silver hair and unlike some who gain weight in their second century of life, Wist is delicate and airy, his face angular, his nose sharp. He's been with me as my butler and assistant for over one hundred years.

I do not smile. I do not nod. "Yes, fine. It was fine."

There is no way I can express to him how fine it was. How coming back feels like splinters against my skin. How Angel has left a hole right in the very center of my heart.

"Very good, sir." Wist does not question me. He knows better when my temper is not full of ho ho hos.

It's full on dark all day and all night at the village now. The polar night is upon us.

However, my castle made of ice reflects all light, starlight, streetlight, my indoor decorative lights. Everything is bright and airy. The cold in the walls is unfelt because of my hearths, one in each room, and the kitchen which is always alive with baking aromas that warm the air in all the halls.

Right now, none of it affects me.

Without a backward glance at Wist, I head up the curving, wide staircase and to my room. I close the door. I crawl into my bed fully clothed, and I sleep. I sleep and sleep until I can't stand it any longer.

When I get up I realize a day and a half has lapsed. I haven't slept that long since the eve after last Christmas following my trip around the world.

It's the middle of the night as I rumble around my kitchen eating just about everything in sight.

Wist appears in the doorway in his flannel pajamas covered in designs of deer and trees, and his long black robe.

"I can help prepare a meal for you, Santa," he offers.

"No. Go back to bed. I'm fine." I dig into a fresh chocolate cake with my fork. No cutting nice, polite pieces. No separate plate. Not for me right now.

The winds of late November roar outside. I've designed my castle so I can hear their calls: angry and frustrated in winter, happy and fey in summer even this far north.

"I can at least make tea. Or cocoa," Wist suggests.

"No. I'm fine. I want to be alone."

Wist stands in the doorway, hesitant to leave. "Did something happen in Alaska?"

"Everything happened in Alaska," I murmur.

"Do you want me to call Jingle at the workshop?" Wist asks.

He knows Jingle is my friend from way back, before Wist worked for me. Wist and I get along, but we aren't confidants. Jingle is my dear friend who also happens to be a great listener.

"I might call him later. Really, Wist, you shouldn't worry about me. Get back to your warm bed."

"Good night, Santa."

"Good night, Wist."

He finally leaves as I dive into the cake.

# Chapter Eleven

## Angel

Royal takes one look at me and says, "You're wearing makeup. You never wear makeup. What's wrong with you?"

"Nothing," I mumble. Before coming to work, I had put on a bit of eyeliner, that's all, and some foundation. It hides the puffiness under my eyes, and the reddened rims.

It's my first day back after taking time off. The sleet is back. It's going to be a slow night with shitty tips, I'm thinking. One more thing to add to my list of sucky things.

Royal has me clean all the tables, even though no one has yet arrived in this weather. Then he sends me to the foyer between the glass doors to make sure it is swept.

I nearly fucking freeze to death before I'm satisfied the floor is indeed clean.

A couple of mountain men come in, dragging snow over my just swept floor.

I toss the broom in the corner with a "fuck it" and grab my tray.

They want beer, the cheapest swill we have, and hot wings served with ranch. They waggle their eyebrows at me as if they've never seen a glittery boy before with no hair on his chest, as if I'm already theirs to eye-fondle and play around with.

When I bring their beers, they each tip me a whole dollar. The food comes later, and that might be another tip, another whole dollar, if they aren't total dicks.

Normally, I'd be smiling and chatting them up, even if I don't like fuzzy, unkempt long beards and the possibility of lice in their hair. But tonight I am distant. I can't seem to focus. No surprise there.

I clomp around the bar like no one cares. Royal keeps giving me the side-eye, but says nothing.

Another patron arrives, a younger, cleaner cut guy, and heads for the bar. I watch him through lowered brows go straight to the seat that was Nic's the second time he came here to watch me at work. That barstool is Nic's. The patron shouldn't be touching it. He most certainly should not be sitting on it.

Of course I know in the time I'd been away many men had probably sat on that stool and ordered drinks and food, and laughed with other men looking for hookups or that one date that would rock their world.

I still can't help but glare at the guy.

Royal waves me over to the bar. "What's wrong, Angelbaby? That guy you kissed in here last week, did he do you wrong?"

Leave it to Royal to hit right on target.

I grumble and shrug. I don't want to talk about Nic. Not to anyone.

"I'm sorry if things didn't work out but you can't keep glaring at the customers."

"What? No one's complaining."

Royal raises his eyebrows. "Well, it's your lack of tips you'll regret when the evening's done."

He is right, of course. Though are those sorts who tip bigger the ruder I am to them. I'd gotten good enough at my job I could read body language and tell who wanted me to treat them wrong, who wanted cute, who had the biggest wallets and who would stiff me.

"I'm beyond caring about tips right now."

"Fuck, text the guy and be done with it," Royal huffs. He walks off to ring in an order.

Text Nic? Of course! I have his number from the few texts we'd exchanged. That connection still exists. Sweat breaks out all over my back at the thought. I can't. I cannot disturb Nic's life like that. He'd clearly stated his terms. We had eleven days and that was that. I agreed to honor those terms.

I grab a rag and start cleaning the already shining bar surface.

The idea of texting won't leave me alone. All night I consider the option. What can I say that won't sound needy and stupid and immature?

The night is slow and Royal talks about sending me home early as the sleet comes down thicker and the parking lot turns to slush. I don't want to go home, though. All I'll do is putter around my condo looking for chores to do to try to take my mind off Nic. To try to keep myself from complete collapse.

104

"Send Joeybear home. He looks utterly bored," I suggest.

Royal glances at the young dark-haired man and shrugs.

In the end, Royal does a rare thing; he closes early. No one is about. Our few customers left long ago. I don't think Royal has hit two hundred tonight. My tips are a measly fifteen bucks. Some nights suck like that.

I go to turn off the neon *open* sign in the front window and shut off the Christmas lights. The empty parking lot comes into full focus, white under the streetlight and gray in the shadows. Slushy. Frozen. It's gonna be a bitch to get out tonight.

I look up at the night sky. Even though the sleet has stopped for now, the stars don't show through the white clouds. It's like the world is encased in a thick nothing. As if we don't really exist.

Royal empties the register. I put the chairs up on the tables and grab the broom and sweep up. Then I go in the back and finish the clean up. There's not much to do.

After I change, I come into the dimly lit bar and Royal is standing by the door looking out. He says, without moving, "I can sense a broken heart a mile away."

"No, you're wrong."

"I'm never wrong. You need to get closure, Angelbaby. Don't ever be afraid to tell another person how you feel. You certainly don't seem to have trouble with that on the job."

"He knows how I feel."

"Really?"

I nod, my reflection bobbing in the darkened window of the door.

"Never assume. It only—"

"Yeah, I know, I know, it makes an ass out of U and me." I roll my eyes.

Royal opens the door to the foyer and I follow him out, tightening my scarf around my neck and pulling down my cap. As we exit and Royal locks the door behind us, a wind kicks up, blowing little pieces of sharp ice into our bodies. My cheeks feel the sting but everything else is thickly covered.

The ice sloshes around or boots as we both make our way to our cars. Once I get inside, I run the engine for a minute until the inside begins to slowly heat up. It's so cold, the heat is barely warm, but it will do for the short drive home.

I wait another minute to see if the heat improves. I take my phone out and open it and go directly to my texts and Nic's messages. I reread them all three times.

It would be so easy to type out a little note. Just to see how he's doing. Just to let him know I still exist. But with my glove off and my bare finger poised over the little keyboard, I chicken out.

I can't face any of the consequences, all of which feel like disaster if he can't return to me. If he doesn't answer, I'll be devastated. Same if he does answer and blows me off with something polite like: *Take care of yourself.* I can't take it. I can't think of him, but I can't stop thinking of him.

I put my phone down and head home, driving slow. No one is on the road tonight. It's spooky and lonely. The trees seem to claw at the roadway, talons silhouetted against the thick gray sky. Everything is colorless. Bleak.

I think about Nic's deer at the cabin. Will they get enough to eat now that Nic has stopped feeding them? I worry about them, and feel silly, but they were so alive and warm surrounding us. Aside from our days spent in bed, feeding the herd of deer is one of my fondest memories of being with Nic.

Tears well up in my eyes. The road grows blurry. No. I won't have it. I won't dissolve. I refuse.

I pull up to my condo. My car only slid once on the way home. No biggie. I walk up the path lined with ice, snow piled high to each side. My windows are dark. The place looks so cold and uninviting, unlike Nic's cabin in the woods.

It's hard for me to go inside all alone and turn on the lights. Everything feels hollow. Off. I have no tree to brighten the place up. Maybe that's what I need. A few decorations. And the scent of baking sugar cookies to come home to.

God, I'm a wreck. I miss Nic so much.

# Chapter Twelve

## Nic

"You have an appointment to visit the workshop today," Wist informs me.

I'm sitting on my couch by the window that faces south, staring at hillocks of snow, the ice crystals reflecting in the brilliant starlight.

Up here in the north, the sky is so clear you can see the entire Milky Way lit up like a postcard picture, the sky so filled with stars they look like mist. It's gorgeous, yet none of it means a thing to me right now.

"Cancel it," I reply.

"Would you rather inspect the stables instead?"

"No."

"And there is the matter of the list."

"The computer can take care of it."

"Sir, you usually like to check it by hand."

"I checked most of it. I started last June."

"Very good, sir."

But there is one name on the list I want to check now. I can't bring myself to do it. Naughty? Or nice? Angelbaby has both sides well covered. He always has and always will. My boy is perfection.

Sometimes I still feel him in my lap, his arms wrapped around my neck. My body remembers everything about him, his weight, the texture of his skin and hair, the brightness of his gold-brown eyes—my body reacts before my mind can catch up. Then I am breathless with wanting. With grief.

I clamp down on my emotions. I need to deal with this. I'm Santa Claus. I can't walk around grumpy all the time. It doesn't fit the suit. Or the role.

I need to stand firm. Angel is a human. No humans are allowed in the village. It's the rule. Granted, it's *my* rule, but I made all my rules for good reasons.

I stare out the window and don't even hear Wist leave.

After a while, my phone flashes, catching my eye. I pick it up. There's a message from Bell, head elf at my stables. I ignore it for now. I scroll through my texts until I read Angel's from over a week ago.

I read through them all twice. There aren't many. I memorize them. I move to the blank line and my fingers hover over the letters to type a message. It would be so easy to contact him. Check up on him. There are no phone towers at the North Pole, but my village has internet and phone service due to a few handy spells I've conducted to open us up, yet still in secret, to this world.

My stomach clenches. I close my eyes and set down the phone.

He is my boy. Or *was* for eleven days. My arms flex, yearning to hold him. My lungs fill as if anticipating his presence. My knees ache to feel his weight in my lap. And my heart—I barely feel it beating right now.

I have so many things I need to take care of before Christmas Eve, which is looming ever closer. But I have little desire or energy to see to the tasks.

I open my eyes and focus again on the white land beneath the intense flashes of starlight. I wonder what Angel is doing right now. Just getting off work at Prancer's? Meeting friends for a late-late dinner or an early morning breakfast?

Going home and sleeping through the day, as I will no doubt do again myself to try to make the pain of missing him disappear for a while?

Dozens of images flood my mind. The flash of white teeth behind Angel's pretty pink lips. Wild blond hair tangling in my hands. The straight line of his jaw. The curve of a flushed cheek. The coins of his pretty dark eyes. Glitter that gets all over me if I take him right after his shift at Prancer's and before he's had a chance to shower.

I can't stop seeing the way he bends for me at the briefest of commands. How his pretty cock lengthens and swells, the shaft several shades darker than his golden skin, the tip pink as early sunset, then darkening to a deep rose just before he comes. And how lovely is that backside, my boy lean-hipped but rounded with the firmness of youth, ass tipped up so I can cup it with my palms, so I can spread it to see the sweet pucker of desire between his cheeks as he gives himself to me with an eagerness that invades my usual calm.

108

Every moment of me taking him is etched into me. My cock is always half-hard, even in my sadness that we are separated now.

After a few hours, with the Milky Way setting toward the southwest, I get up and wander the halls of my home.

Upstairs, down a long hall that culminates in my master bedroom, are doors that lead to closets, a bathroom, and two guestrooms. And near the end, before reaching my door, are two more suite-sized rooms.

Both have signs over the archways that say: *Toy Room.*

One is ajar, and through the crack in the door I see rows upon rows of toys my elves have made in their workshop that I have kept instead of given away. Dolls that are works of art. Cars, trains, boats, games. Stuffed bears, cats, dogs, dragons and unicorns shining with gilt. Rocking horses. Bicycles. Jewelry making kits. Art kits. Model rockets. Toy houses. It is my collection. My hoard which represents the best of my talented elves.

I keep this room tidy. Elf housekeepers dust it every day.

The second toy room has a little sign underneath that says: *Authorized Personnel Only.*

The door to that room is double locked. I have the key on a small chain in my pocket. Always on me. But that room has not been opened in probably fifty years. I don't have need of it. But I keep it anyway. A room that contains my many secrets, my fantasies, my fetishes.

I move on to my master bedroom. Everything is perfect, thanks to Wist's foresight. His ability to read me and my moods is what has made me keep him on here, while other elf workers come and go at my whim or theirs.

My bed is turned down with new white sheets beneath a folded-back red comforter. Candles are lit in crystal jars and burning on nightstands on either side of the head of the bed. Two squares of foil-wrapped chocolate mints grace the centers of two white pillows.

My white, faux-fur rugs are freshly vacuumed. The en-suite bathroom, door open, glistens with its bright mirrors and track lighting, and smells like peaches.

All the luxury registers on my mind but gives me no pleasure.

I sit on the edge of the bed and remove my boots. It seems I've just gotten up, but actually an entire day has passed, and me having accomplished nothing.

I take off my shirt and slacks. I let them fall where they may, my usual habit of folding my clothes and stacking them forgotten. Wearing only my red satin boxers, I slip my long legs beneath the covers. I lie back, waving the lights off, leaving the bathroom light on so it's not entirely dark. There is enough darkness outside during polar night that I like a little comforting light as I sleep.

But sleep at this juncture eludes me.

I close my eyes. Open them. Close them again.

Damn it. Angel should be here. Curled at my side. Or on his side with his back pressed against my chest, his buttocks nestled at my crotch. I should be nosing into his hair, inhaling his sweet scent.

Naked, we should be entwined until neither of us can feel where one leaves off and the other begins. We should be together like the two sides of a ribbon combined to make a bow at the top of a Christmas present.

I open my eyes. My phone sits dark on my nightstand, its glass screen blank. I take a deep breath and reach out.

I swipe the phone on and look again and again at our few texts. We never utilized that option overly much because most of our free time was spent together.

Slowly, as if in a dream of love I cannot control, a fantasy plan forms in my mind. An insane plan. A risky plan. An idea that could threaten my entire secret world.

First, I put in a call to the stables where the elves jump to my every command. I have no worries they can do all I ask in a short time.

The next call is to the workshop. I spell out my need. It's rare. It's expensive. This type of gift is not my standard fare, but something given from human to human. Do they have it?

Jingle, on the other end of the line, assures me they do.

Now I sit staring at Angel's texts again. Gathering every ounce of courage I have, I begin to type my message. It isn't that I don't want to do this. I have enough love to see this through. It's merely my fear. I've never done this before. I've never loved a human.

My text to Angel is short. I deliberately keep it benign and mysterious.

*After your shift tonight, I will be at the cabin for a short time. Meet me there?*

I go to my closet and search through all my clothes, my palm landing on one hanger. I take it out. It's an Armani tuxedo that looks shiny black but is actually blood red when the light hits the silk-wool blend just right.

I take out a crisp, starched white shirt and a deep red bowtie. It doesn't have sequins on it like the one Angelbaby wears at work, but it matches the handkerchief that goes in the left breast pocket.

I begin to dress.

# Chapter Thirteen

## Angel

Royal has been frowning at me all night. It's not because he hates me, or is unhappy with my work. No. He loves to meddle. And I won't let him.

He has hounded me for two nights now to text "that boyfriend you're pining over." When I refuse, or ignore him, it makes him grumpy. As if his role of boss has transcended from telling me what to do at work to telling me what to do with my life.

Infuriating.

Yet part of me knows he's right. I need to do something. I'm clumsy all night. I drop things. I break two whole trays of glasses. I mess up the change on some orders.

Royal's really a good guy. He does not threaten to take any of it out of my pay as he usually does. I think he feels somewhat sorry for me. He's got his live-in boyfriend and his life while I'm some aimless kitten tossed around in the snow. He can't help but want to dust me off, warm me up, and get me back on my feet.

I don't tell him about the dream I've had for two nights in a row.

It's about Nic. Of course.

In my dream, Nic is surrounded by snow. Behind him is an array of lights, like a little city twinkling in the background. Nic wears all red, and he looks bigger than he really is.

I'm standing in front of him in only my pajamas, and the stars overhead are like another city so big and huge and filled with so many beings, ancient and new, from every sun it cannot be fathomed. Not by humans. Not by anyone, really, except in the realm of fiction.

In the dream, an icy wind blows my hair, but I don't feel the cold. Nic beckons me. He holds out his arms.

I woke both times from that dream feeling as if Nic's arms surrounded me from behind. As if we were together and never really parted.

I would lie still in my bed and feel the caress of his palm on my stomach. I even smelled him: woodsy, peppermint, mince pie.

The connection between us exists. For me. But does he feel it as well? I'm too chicken to text him. Every time I try, the tears begin. I'm not ready.

That's why it's such a surprise when I check my phone on my break and see a text sitting there from Nic. I blink hard. At first my vision blurs and can't read it. Then I want to look away. Not know for a few minutes. Wonder what it says. Is it a final goodbye? Does he want me back?

But that lasts only a few seconds. I have to read it. I need to know.

*After your shift tonight, I will be at the cabin for a short time. Meet me there?*

That's it. Nothing more. No hearts. No X's and O's. Nothing to tell me he misses me. Maybe he is only returning some item I've left behind, I tell myself. Maybe the meeting is the final goodbye.

I'm so confused and broken up inside that it stands to reason I can only see a negative outcome to this.

My stomach turns over. My heart hammers in my chest. For a moment, I can't breathe. It's too much.

"No," I say aloud. Then, "Please, no."

I can't do this to myself. I can't see Nic again only to walk away. Again. I'll surely die of a trampled heart.

But then the blood surges in my veins. The anticipation begins. The voice in my head starts going and going. *You'll get to see him! He wants to meet! He hasn't already forgotten you. It's a tiny chance he still wants you.*

Of course that voice is loudest, and automatically I start considering if the clothes I wore to work are pretty enough. I need to look my best. I need to be perfect when I see him again.

I think about answering the text now. Telling him yes, I will come. Telling him all my thoughts over the last two days.

I don't do it. I want him to wait for me. I want him to wonder. It's not punishment. But in a way, maybe it is. Maybe it's manipulative. Make him wait. Make him wonder. Does he get to see me or not? Will I show? Or will I stay away?

A part of me grimaces in a sort of negative pleasure at causing him to not know my decision until I walk up to him. Until my gaze meets his.

The rest of my shift seems endless. Royal keeps sighing and rolling his eyes, but keeps his mouth shut. I'm too keyed up to tell him—or anyone—about the text.

Tonight Prancer's is more lively the later it gets. It hasn't snowed or sleeted today, so more people are out. But it's all a blur to me. I am displaced from reality. Seeing Nic and all his gorgeous, caring smiles, feeling the ways he held me, blushing at all the intimate memories makes me feel far outside my body. I am floating above myself the rest of my shift, looking down at myself going through the motions of waiting on customers.

I watch the clock intently. The time never seems to change.

Finally, my shift is over. I don't close tonight. I wonder if Nic knows. My hours can vary. Did he spy tonight? Was he keeping track of my shifts?

I like to imagine it. I like to believe he's thinking about me as much as I've been thinking about him.

When I change out of my leather pants and put on my jeans, they look ratty, old. The sweater I wore to work tonight is worn at the elbows. I wasn't caring what I put on, not paying attention these last couple of days to my fashion sense.

I glance in the mirror above the sink in the employee bathroom. The style of my hair is okay, groomed well enough for being on the job, but there is a little too much glitter falling around me, sticking to my sweater, and I feel sweaty and gross.

It's nerves, but who cares? I shouldn't. But I do. It's Nic, and I care about everything he might think about me.

It's two degrees Fahrenheit outside. I get in my car and wait for it to warm up inside and out. I close my eyes and try to calm my thumping heart. Relax my muscles. Breathe.

I pull out onto the black ribbon of highway that leads to the other side of town. Summerwood.

As I drive, I think about the first night I met Nic, how I learned he had walked to Prancer's from his cabin. It's pretty far. Even though he told me he doesn't feel the cold, how he didn't freeze to death is beyond me.

As I approach the turn off to his cabin, I go slower and slower. It's late enough that I meet no oncoming traffic. Everyone is snug and safe in their homes and their beds. Everyone but me. And Nic.

Finally, I turn. My tires hit a muddy patch as I cut the corner close and edge the shoulder. Something bright catches my eye as the road straightens. A glow just beyond the hill where the cabin is. It's really bright. As if the cabin is on fire.

The closer I get, the brighter the glow gets. White and almost flickering. A halo surrounding the area.

I pass over the small hill and the cabin comes into view. All around it is a forest of electric trees. Most have white lights, but a few interspersed are gold, blue, red and green. There must be two dozen or more. Lighting up the snow. Lighting up the sky.

The front of the cabin blazes with its usual lights outlining the frame.

Among the trees, deer walk about. The very deer Nic and I fed for eleven days in a row. And standing right in the middle of it all is Nic.

Nic wears no parka or scarf or hat. He looks like a guy right out of a romance novel, clad in a black tuxedo with a red bowtie. The glow of all the lights surrounds him. His hair falls perfectly about his face, gold, gold-brown, bronze.

Nic turns to watch as I pull up the drive and my lights catch him. For a moment, his tuxedo turns blood-red. He looks almost supernatural.

My heart stopped many seconds ago. Seeing him is amazing and difficult and makes me feel out of control. He's so beautiful. I want to cry and laugh at the same time. He's set all this up. Just for me. It can't be because he wants to say goodbye again.

I pull slowly up the driveway, watching to make sure the deer stay put, and that I don't scare them with the rumble of my car.

Nic follows me with his gaze until I stop. I leave the engine on for a few seconds, then turn it off.

Everything goes quiet inside the car. I have no music playing, nothing. Slowly, I open the door.

The outside cold hits me hard, but I ignore it. My love burns too brightly to let frozen air affect me right now, to let the pain in my lungs give me more than a passing thought.

My breath steams in front of me and I stand, shutting the door behind me.

All of the lights hit my senses at once. And the deer so peaceful and serene. And Nic, solid and otherworldly, as if he is king of the cold and has come to me out of a fairy tale to set all this up. It's magnificent. No one could do all this on such short notice. No one but Nic, of course.

What sort of man is he? The most giving and caring. Handsome and kind. The daddy I've dreamed of since I was sixteen and felt deep inside me I wanted to some day be somebody's boy.

That is the sort of man Nic is. And I can't pretend I don't want to beg him to take me wherever he goes. I can't close myself off from the burst of huge emotion inside me.

For all the chaos that now rules my mind, my voice comes out soft and shy. "Nic?"

"Hello, Angelbaby."

# Chapter Fourteen

## Nic

Surges of adrenaline stab my limbs and whirl through my stomach.

My beautiful boy.

He's standing right in front of me.

It feels as if a million years have passed since I held him, and yet also as if no time at all has transpired.

For a long moment, Angel stands as if frozen next to his car. But before my next blink, suddenly he's running, snow kicking up behind him, the deer rustling and bucking at the sudden motion, moving off into the light tree forest by the sides of the cabin.

The snow hinders Angel's progress, but he leaps through it, my young, lithe boy, and as I hold out my arms to him he jumps up.

I catch him as he nearly topples me over, and my first laugh in two days rings out into the night.

Angel closes his arms about my neck and clings to my waist with his thighs. I have nowhere to put my hands except on his jeans-clad ass. It feels so right to be holding him again. As if he's a puzzle piece that's been missing from my life for years.

He buries his face in my neck. And I whisper into his glittered hair. "Baby."

His body against mine goes into a rapid shudder, and I realize he's crying. I throw back my head and gaze up at the tremble of stars above. We are one. We are all one. But this baby is mine.

"It's all right, Angelbaby. I'm here."

"Please don't leave me." He sniffs delicately. "Please."

After a while, he lowers himself to his feet, but I don't take my hands away from him. Standing in the snow among the light trees, we remain chest to chest.

"I won't leave you," I tell him. I swallow hard. How to show him my world? One baby step at a time.

"You'll stay, then?"

"No."

His body stiffens.

"I'm taking you with me."

He looks up at me, sleek eyebrows disappearing into the locks of his hair. "Taking me? Where?"

"Now that is the big question, isn't it?"

He frowns. "Why is that the big question? I already know you live in the north. Near Nunavut." His frown turns placid, his pink lips turning up.

"Because it's very out of the way and distant from the area you're used to. I didn't want to take you away from what you know."

"Is that why you left without saying goodbye?" he asks.

I can only nod. The pain in his voice is too much.

Angel takes a deep breath. "I dreamed of a city, like it was lost in the tundra, but you were there. And you never felt the cold, just like now, and now—now I remember something else about the dream. You had a big car. Red. Like a giant truck. Or Hummer. Something like that." His smile widens.

"You dreamed all that?"

He bobs his head up and down, leaning against my chest.

"It is—uh—rather accurate."

"So is that where we're going?" he asks.

"Yes. It does seem you are uncannily accurate."

"I've always been able to sense things about people. It's not hard. It's just energy, right? There's been something you've been trying to tell me all this time, but you couldn't. It's okay. You don't have to say anything more. I'll keep your secrets, Nic. All of them. I promise from the depths of my very soul. Just take me with you."

I'm stunned. But why would I ever think my boy could be anything other than extraordinary? He's mine. That means he's more than special. He's my match. My mate. We're connected.

"I can't leave you."

"Good." Angel puts his arms around me. "You're so warm. I don't even feel the cold when I'm touching you."

"Ah, that's part of my magic."

Voice muffled in my chest with a laugh, I say, "I missed you so much."

I hold him to me for a while. Finally, I step back. His palms scrape along my tux jacket, reluctant to let go.

"Just stand there a moment," I say.

Angel looks up at me, hands at his sides. I look down at the thick layer of snow we're standing in. For me it's not cold, and I go down on one knee.

Angel gasps. "Nic! Daddy, your beautiful tuxedo is going to get all wet."

"It'll dry," I say.

I reach into my pocket and pull out a small, black velvet box. "I have a present for you."

Angels face flushes all over. He puts his gloved hands to his mouth, his eyebrows moving up.

"It's very early for us to be saying some things to each other. I know it is. But I love you, sweetheart."

Angel gulps and his eyes fill with tears.

"I mean it. I want you to have this to show you my commitment to taking this relationship as far as we can. Together."

I hold out the box so he can see it, then open it.

Angel lowers one arm and lets me place the box on his upturned hand. He stares.

Inside is a band of finest platinum. Elfin crafted. Around the band are sapphires laid out in snowflake patterns.

"It's breathtaking," Angel says, voice all air and steam coming from between his sweet lips.

"It connects us. This ring," I say, and my throat begins to close up. I've never given anyone a ring before, despite rumors to the contrary. I have never been engaged, never married.

"We're already connected," Angel says.

He lifts his hand and bites off his glove. Then he takes the ring and places it on his left ring finger. "It fits perfectly!" He waves his hand and the ring sparkles in the brilliant lights that surround us. Then he comes forward and throws his arms around my neck, hugging me so tight I am overwhelmed.

"Daddy, I love you!"

Those are the words I never thought I'd hear after leaving him two days ago. Words I never gave him the chance to say. Until now.

We hug for a long minute. Finally, I step back.

"And now, it's time to go."

"Go? Already? But I haven't packed."

"We will send for anything you wish. We do have delivery service where we are going."

"I—I have to let Royal know. I have to--"

"You will have internet and phone service as well. You can still stay connected to anyone you wish. You'll simply live with me from now on."

"And be your boy?"

Flames begin in the center of my belly. "Yes. And be my boy."

Angel looks around. "But I don't see your car? Are we going to an airport? Are we taking my car?"

I shake my head. "Do you trust me, baby?"

Slowly, he nods.

I reach out and take his ungloved hand in mine. "Walk with me."

He looks up at me as I guide him through the light tree forest, around the side of the cabin and out toward the back where the woods begin.

"We're going out there in the woods? At night?"

"Yes. You'll be fine. You aren't cold, are you?"

"Strangely, no. Not as long as you're touching me."

"It's only a short walk."

"Okay." His voice is trusting and young.

We walk through trees for about five minutes in silence. Hand in hand. Finally, we reach the clearing I've chosen. There, my reindeer wait. And my giant red sleigh gleaming in the starlight.

Angel stops, yanking my arm back. I watch him as he blinks and blinks. Not trusting his vision.

"It's not a Hummer," I say. "But your dream was very close."

"You set this up. It's brilliant," Angel says.

"Set it up?"

He glances at me. "It's beautiful. What a beautiful gift. You must be, like, really wealthy to bring off something like this."

"I am. But it's not a set up. This is how we are getting home."

"What?"

"I live at the North Pole. And I'm taking you with me."

"This is a trick?"

"No. My sweet boy. I would never trick you. I know it's a lot, but I hope in due time you can accept that I'm—I'm somewhat different from you."

120

Without a word, Angel crunches through the snow and walks up to the sleigh. He touches it and his ring shines. He runs his palm over the curving edge where the little door opens for entry into what I call the cockpit.

"Would you like to go for a ride?" I ask.

Angel glances at the eight reindeer, then back at me. "You're real?"

"Always was," I reply.

"It's not possible."

"It is right before your eyes," Nic says.

"But—but--"

"I understand it will take a while for you to process. But in the meantime, everything's ready. How about that ride?"

"I think I'm dreaming again, but yes. Fuck yes! I want to go for a ride!"

# Chapter Fifteen

## Angel

It must be that I'm dreaming. Since I'm totally sober, it's the only explanation.

But what a dream.

Nic. Short for Nicholas? Saint Nicholas?

My daddy is Santa Claus?

I don't understand any of this, but I love it. And I love Nic. He's all that matters. I'll play any fantasy with him in the hope that everything I want to have happen between us comes true.

"Fuck yes I want to go for a ride!"

Nic comes forward and opens the little door that leads into the open sleigh.

"We'll freeze to death for sure."

Nic smiles. "Trust me?"

"Yes." I trust him completely. Daddy Santa would never allow me to come to harm.

"I have a technology within me. It might seem like magic to you."

"Taught to you by your grandmother. I remember," I say. "You told me you're a witch. A sorcerer."

"Yes. I can protect us with a bubble against the wind and the cold. And trust that also these reindeer come from the same realm as I. They *can* fly."

I let out a whoosh of air and a low moan. This is not happening, and yet it is.

Nic assists me into the sleigh. The bench across the front is upholstered in shining black leather. In front of me is a dash with knobs shaped like the elongated old-fashioned kinds of Christmas lights. These look like they lead to drawers, or doors to hidden compartments. Otherwise, the sleigh is very simple. The reins connecting the deer are neatly tucked into notches and tied off in a bow.

Nic gets in beside me and closes the little door.

"Are you ready?" he asks.

My stomach feels like it's in my chest. I'm terrified and excited at the same time. I don't feel like I'm in a trance. I am aware. I have all my wits. Yet I keep thinking this must be a dream.

I watch in a daze as Nic takes the reins in hand. Then he calls out two unbelievable words.

"Dash away!"

The deer begin to move. Soon they break into a run, all in sync, and the sleigh slides noiselessly across the snow. The ride is smooth, like gliding, and then as I watch, the deer lift off the ground.

I grab Nic around the waist but I can't take my eyes off them. They lift up, their legs still moving in unison as if they are running on air, and the sleigh tilts up. And then we're flying.

I yell. Not any word, or anything comprehensible. Just a noise. I can't help but grin. For a moment I feel the wind on my face, but Nic takes the reins in one hand and makes a motion with the other and warmth blasts against my face as if a heater has been turned on. It must be the bubble he mentioned.

"We won't be seen," he says, matter of fact. "As soon as we clear the woods and go a little higher, a cloak activates."

"A cloak?"

He turns to me with a huge smile. "Have you never seen Star Trek?"

"Have you?" I ask, meeting his grin with my own.

"Every single episode, movie and series. Even the stupid cartoon."

I laugh out loud. "Me, too!"

\*

We fly for what seems like a long time surrounded by stars. At least an hour. Sometimes quick storms seem to pass right through us filled with ice and snow. But I don't feel any of that. I'm constantly trying to wrap my mind around this inconceivable reality I've somehow landed in.

The reindeer are beautiful with their full antler racks and graceful moves on the air. They are powerful beings, beyond normal, alien compared to the deer I've seen and fed.

123

"How long does it take to get to the North Pole in this?" I ask, expecting it to be hours.

"With the time slip I'm using, only a few more minutes."

"Time slip? What?"

"I can teach you all of it once we're home."

Home. I wonder if it is like the city of lights I saw in my dream two nights in a row.

"No human has ever been to my village before," Nic begins. "It's not allowed."

"Then, what will happen when you bring me in?"

"Nothing. The rule is mine alone. And mine to break."

"I have so many questions, Nic."

"I know," he replies. "Would you like to hold the reins?"

"Can I?"

"Of course."

I'm scared and exhilarated as Nic hands over the leather strips to me. I take them reverently. The deer don't react. They keep to their course, true and strong.

"They all know where they're going," Nic assures me.

"Are their names really Dasher and Dancer and Prancer--" I stop before going any further, feeling like I'm making a fool of myself.

But Nic surprises me when he says, "Yes."

It's all too amazing for words.

Little bells jingle along the harnesses, all the way up to the lead deer.

As I'm intent on the deer and the way they seem to be flying straight up into the stars, Nic says, "There it is."

I look up at him and follow his gaze. Down below us and ahead lies a huge snowflake made of light right in the middle of a tundra.

As we fly closer and Nic takes back the reins, I see it's actually a little village with lanes that extend outward from the center, all lined with streetlights. Cabins and buildings dot the landscape, all orderly. At one edge of the snowflake's arm is a gleaming white castle that looks as if it is made right out of the ice. It's lit up from inside and out, giving it a silver-blue sheen.

"That's where we're headed," Nic says, pointing to the castle.

"That's where you live?"

"It is."

It will be my home, too, now. I have been captured by a swirl of ice and a dreamy Santa Claus. I can never go home, I think to myself. No one will ever believe my stories.

The deer and sleigh circle the village, giving me a closer glimpse of sweet, frosted cabins nestled in snowdrifts, and larger buildings as well. One, Nic points out, is the workshop.

Well, hell yes, there would be a workshop. Santa's Village wouldn't be complete without one.

Another building is the stables. Yet another is an indoor mall.

We circle toward the castle now. It has a tipped rooftop lined with little towers, like a fairytale castle.

The sleigh drifts down as if weightless and circles the castle before bringing us into a snow-framed lane that leads right up to the front.

Two men in thick parkas with long tailed knit caps come up the walkway from the front. They open the little door of the sleigh.

"Welcome back, Santa."

They glance at me.

"This is Angel," says Nic. "He is my guest for an indefinite amount of time."

"Yes, sir."

"Angel, this is Wist. He lives in the castle. And this is Ever. He lives down the road with his husband on the other side of the park."

They both nod and bow slightly in my direction.

Elves, I think. These are elves. They look like normal humans; I'm relieved I won't feel totally out of place.

The elf named Ever greets each deer by name and pats him on the side of the neck.

As Nic and I disembark, Wist bows us toward the castle door, which is framed in colored lights and has a big golden wreath on the front.

Nic turns. "Ever, I trust you to take the reindeer all back to the stables and make sure they get extra candy canes for dessert."

Ever grins and gives Nic a thumbs up.

Nic whisks me inside where I am greeted by a mass of lights and decorations. Candlelight gleams from just about every surface. A huge tree stands before a tall, curving staircase.

I look at Nic with my mouth open.

Nic shrugs. "I can't stop collecting holiday décor."

"It's all so beautiful. And overwhelming."

In a whirlwind, Nic gives me a tour. The front room is like a Christmas card with a huge hearth, another Christmas tree, and stockings over the fireplace. The kitchen is big enough to skate in, with two ovens and two islands.

"You know I like to bake," Nic says.

The staircase is trimmed with holly. Mistletoe hangs over the landing. Lights spiral the rail. Everything smells fresh and pine-scented.

Down a long hall, Nic shows me room after room. "Guest rooms," he explains, "though I don't have many. Wist has his own room down at the other end."

One of the rooms is huge and filled with toys.

Another is also labeled, *Toy Room,* but Nic says he'll show me that one later. I can see it is locked.

The cherry on top is Nic's master bedroom. Everything is red and white with green accents. The bed is red. The walls are trapped white ice like gleaming crystal, yet it's warm inside. The curtains against the white walls are dark red. The candle holders all along the shelves of the headboard and on the nightstands are emerald.

On one side of the room, a door opens to mirrors and sinks. A bathroom.

I look at the bed with mountains of pillows nearly toppling over themselves. It looks so inviting.

I try not to yawn. I am too excited to sleep, but realize I'm exhausted. Everything has been overwhelming to my senses until I can't take any more. I blink hard. I put a hand over my mouth to cover another yawn that threatens to overtake me.

Nic puts an arm across my shoulders. "I'm so glad you're here with me."

"Me, too."

Those two words I utter hold all my emotion. My affection. My feelings of falling in love harder with each moment I spend with Nic.

Nic squeezes me to him and says, "And now I think it's bedtime for naughty boys who can't stop yawning at my magnificent abode."

"I'm not!" I protest.

But before I can say another word, Nic picks me up and cradles me in his arms. He takes me into the bathroom where he runs me a

126

bath and bathes me through all the bubbles. The scent of the soap is spicy with a little bit of apple thrown in. It hypnotizes me yet I don't want to sleep. I want to stay awake and aware so I can be with Nic.

But he won't have any of it. He doesn't tease me as he usually does when he gives me baths. He washes me off and then dries me with big towels, then carries me to his bed.

I'm naked as he places beneath the covers.

Nic strips, carefully hanging every piece of his tux before walking naked to climb into the big red bed beside me. He waves his hand to make the lights go out, but candles flicker in their green glass jars, making undersea-like shadows on the walls.

Nic pulls me to him, and I rub myself against him, my cock half-hard, my eyes half-closed.

He brings a pillow against his chest where I lay my head.

"I missed you so much." He kisses the top of my head. He rubs my side and back, down to my ass, caressing me with reverence. With love.

I let the tears fall, wetting the pillow, as Nic says, "My sweet boy."

"I'm finally home," I say.

Nic lifts my chin so his mouth can meet mine, and he kisses me like no other man ever has.

That's when I know, through and through, I'm truly his now. And he'll never again let me go.

# Epilogue

## Angel

For twenty-four hours Nic will be gone.

It's Christmas Eve morning and he's already left for the stables. I'm on my own now until noon on Christmas day. I already miss him.

It's not like there's nothing to do. I have the run of the ice castle. There are video games, movies, computers, puzzles, cookies to bake, and my own presents for Nic I still need to wrap.

What do you get a man who has everything, or the magic to attain whatever he might be missing?

Well, not much. I got him an ugly Christmas sweater which I'm going to make him wear to bed. And a giant Christmas blanket covered in silhouette designs of sleighs pulled by reindeer across forests and full moons and snowy mountain peaks.

Nic wears a silver necklace with a key on it around his neck. I order another one for him, only this one has a charm on it of sleigh made of sterling silver.

What else can I do for him? I have only these gifts plus myself to give. I figure it's enough.

Nic had my stuff packed and delivered soon after I moved in. I sent Royal an email that I had to move suddenly so I could no longer work at Prancer's. I still had contact through the Internet with my friends and family. No one would report me as a missing person.

Today and tonight, Nic is driving his reindeer and sleigh through time slips all throughout Christmas Eve, visiting all parts of the world that welcome his myth and magic. I wanted to accompany him, but he told me my mind wasn't ready yet for that sort of long journey. I realize he's probably right.

I am restless the entire day of Christmas Eve. I try to occupy myself with all the entertainment at my fingertips. But by midnight, I'm still not tired. I don't want to sleep. And I am even more restless.

I find myself by the big tree staring at the gilt-wrapped gifts beneath. So many of them have my name on them.

Nic spares me nothing. What else is giving me?

Curious, I step forward. Wist has long gone off to bed, so he's not around to shake an elfin finger at me.

I know I'm not supposed to touch these gifts until Nic returns. He implored me not to peek. It's wrong. It's naughty. But I have no will power. I cannot stop myself from stooping, then kneeling, then pulling out the stacks of gifts addressed: *Angelbaby*.

I hesitate over the first gift on top. But why? What will Nic do if I peek? Punish me? I live for his spankings, and all the other things he does to me to make me the naughty boy I am.

I undo the bow, carefully, so I can re-wrap it and get away with my snooping.

Inside the first box: socks. Socks?

I throw them over my shoulder thinking, what the fuck? Hell, I'll put them back later.

The next box contains a new scarf. It's a very pretty blue with white snowflakes. Silk and wool. I set that aside as well.

More gifts await.

The next gift is a bit better. More private. It's a polished wooden rack that holds five bottles of different flavored lube. Orange. Chocolate. Peppermint. Sugar cookie. Green apple.

My cheeks ache from my wide grin. I hope we'll get to use each one. Perhaps all in one night.

The next box contains a similar rack. This one holds five differently shaped butt plugs. Silver. Gold. Onyx. Cobalt. Jade. Each one has a large jewel at the base, all of different colors, which will glimmer and flicker against my asshole once the item is fully in place. I like the idea of jewels next to my jewels. I chuckle aloud at the thought. My daddy takes great care of me.

The next package contains underwear. At first glance, one would throw that gift over with the socks to land in the forgotten *gifts you need* pile. But not these.

I pick up the first pair of pearly silver silk. It is skimpy and on closer inspection, has a hole in the back where your ass can poke through. The front is a pouch barely big enough to contain a man's junk. I know *I* won't fit in these, but I'll love trying.

The next is red satin trimmed in white faux-fur. Santa undies! Bikini style. I hold them to my face, feeling how soft they are against my cheek.

The next pair is green. Straps crisscross to form the shape from the elastic waistband to the elastic leg holes. But the X's those straps make are huge and wide. If I put those on, my cock would pop out between the X's and my back end would stretch them to the breaking point. Nothing will be hidden when I wear them.

The box is filled with half a dozen more pairs of underwear, some lacy, some with flowers, some with stars. They are all tiny, not at all practical. Definitely not warm underwear to wear during the winter months.

But I don't need warm. I have Nic. When he touches me, I blaze.

As I reach the bottom of the box of undies, I see a thick roll of paper tied with a bow. It almost looks like a scroll. I slide the red bow off and unroll the paper.

It's a handwritten note!

Eagerly, I begin to read.

*Dear Angelbaby,*

*If you are reading this and I am not by your side, there will be no doubt that you have broken my rule and peeked at your presents before I arrive home on Christmas day.*

*You were well informed this was strictly forbidden by me, your daddy.*

*You are probably now sitting in the middle of a pile of wrapping paper, bows and presents like the naughtiest of boys, wondering how you can fix this. How you can wrap them all back up and place them in perfect order so I will never know.*

*Rest assured, this is not so. I have installed various security devices in random ornaments throughout the tree. You are already caught live on cameras from different angles. I can see them on my phone from wherever I am in the world tonight.*

*Your only saving grace is to finish what you started. Your mess will be my delight when I return by noon tomorrow.*

*Here are my instructions as to what you will do. Deviate from them, and you will be sorry.*

*Go toward the center of the tree's base and find a small box I have hidden there in the skirts. When you open it, you will find the key I always wear around my neck. This key fits the lock on the toy room—the one that says **Authorized Personnel Only**—on the second floor.*

*After you shower and are thoroughly shaved and clean, you will take these things I have given you and enter this locked room and disrobe. You will then prepare yourself—again thoroughly—for me, and insert the plug of your choice. I myself love the gold one, but you may choose.*

*Next, don the backless, silver underwear.*

*In the room you will see a bed of finest cottons and silks with the softest of mattresses. You will also see, on the wall, a collection of paddles in all types of wood and of all colors. Pick one. Place it at the foot of the bed along with the lube of your choice. You will then get into the bed and into position. That means hands and knees, boy, facing the headboard, ass up, eyes down.*

*You will hold that position until I arrive. If your position falters, or you fall asleep, your punishment will be even more severe. You have permission only to get up and use the toilet or get a drink of water.*

*If you move or squirm, if you become roused and seek the need to alleviate your frustration, you must deny yourself. I do not give you permission to take yourself in hand and satisfy your desires. If you cannot control yourself, you will find an array of cock cages—yes, I collect them—on the shelf over the bed. Use one if you must.*

*Make yourself hard. Keep yourself in position. Wait for me.*

*Love, Daddy*

I look at the mess on the floor all around me. I glance back at the letter, all handwritten in fancy calligraphy in my daddy's own hand. I read it a second time. Then a third.

I take the key on the necklace from the last present and put it around my neck. I grab up my gifts—except for the socks—and leave the rest of the mess, that way as he walks through the front door he'll know what I've been up to. And exactly where to find me. Although, of course, he's seen it all on his cameras.

I will do everything he says. Like the good boy I can be, and the naughty boy I am, I will be ready for him.

131

Santa is coming for Christmas.

———

# Santa's Naughty Boy Bonus Scene:

## *The Toy Room*

by

**Wendy Rathbone**

# The Toy Room

# 1.

## *Angelbaby*

Dear Angelbaby,

*If you are reading this and I am not by your side, there will be no doubt that you have broken my rule and peeked at your presents before I arrive home on Christmas day.*

*You were well informed this was strictly forbidden by me, your daddy.*

*You are probably now sitting in the middle of a pile of wrapping paper, bows and presents like the naughtiest of boys, wondering how you can fix this. How you can wrap them all back up and place them in perfect order so I will never know.*

*Rest assured, this is not so. I have installed various security devices in random ornaments throughout the tree. You are already caught live on cameras from different angles. I can see them on my phone from wherever I am in the world tonight.*

*Your only saving grace is to finish what you started. Your mess will be my delight when I return by noon tomorrow.*

*Here are my instructions as to what you will do. Deviate from them, and you will be sorry.*

*Go toward the center of the tree's base and find a small box I have hidden there in the skirts. When you open it, you will find the key I always wear around my neck. This key fits the lock on the toy room—the one that says **Authorized Personnel Only**—on the second floor.*

*After you shower and are thoroughly shaved and clean, you will take these things I have given you and enter this locked room and disrobe. You will then prepare yourself—again thoroughly—for me, and insert the plug of your choice. I myself love the gold one, but you may choose.*

*Next, don the backless, silver underwear.*

*In the room you will see a bed of finest cottons and silks with the softest of mattresses. You will also see, on the wall, a collection of paddles in all types of wood and of all colors. Pick one. Place it at the foot of the bed along with the lube of your choice. You will then get into the bed and into position. That means hands and knees, boy, facing the headboard, ass up, eyes down.*

*You will hold that position until I arrive. If your position falters, or you fall asleep, your punishment will be even more severe. You have permission only to get up and use the toilet or get a drink of water.*

*If you move or squirm, if you become roused and seek the need to alleviate your frustration, you must deny yourself. I do not give you permission to take yourself in hand and satisfy your desires. If you cannot control yourself, you will find an array of cock cages—yes, I collect them—on the shelf over the bed. Use one if you must.*

*Make yourself hard. Keep yourself in position. Wait for me.*

*Love, Daddy*

\*

I've been a very naughty boy.

I've opened presents before Christmas day, and before Nic has had the chance to return from his long night of delivering gifts around the world on Christmas Eve.

I've done it now. I truly deserve any punishment Nic decides to give me.

As per Nic's instructions in the note I found at the bottom of a box of sexy satin and lace underwear (so many pairs to choose from!) I have showered and shaved, including below the waist. I have prepped myself with fingers and oil until I am open and slick in back, hard in front.

In a loose, satin robe, I now take the key to Santa's secret adult toy room and let myself in.

As much as I have let Nic know how open I am to bedroom play in all ways with him, in the month we have been together he hasn't let me see this locked room. Until now.

I enter and turn on the light.

I stand before an elaborate bedroom.

The bed in the center against the main wall has a black lacquer headboard and deep red spread with white fuzzy trim. It is larger than a king-size bed, no doubt custom made. It has a red canopy to match the comforter. The top is rimmed with silver ball ornaments that reflect the light.

On the wall left of the bed hang various paddles and whips. All look brand new, never used. Large and small. Red, green, natural wood and one that is hot pink and lined with holes. That one looks like it would smart! I can't help but wonder if the holes would leave little white dents in the skin of my ass.

To the right of the bed hang fancy chains and cuffs and a couple more whips. I shudder. I am not sure about the whips, but they're fun to contemplate.

A shelf over the headboard holds even more intriguing toys and I move forward onto thick white rugs to get a closer look. There stands a collection of cock cages, some square, some tubular, all with thin chains attached to rings and plugs. They look like jewelry. For your junk.

Santa's note says I am to use one if I can't control myself while I am waiting for him. I'm not sure I even know how to put one on!

But the idea of all that metal pressed against me, glimmering against my skin, ringing my shaft and my balls, chains looping through my thighs and hooking to my hole with a pretty little plug, makes my skin heat all over.

I want to play. As I've told Nic, I want everything with him. Even if it makes me nervous—I glance at the whips—I want to try.

I move toward shelves on one side wall.

Dildos line the top shelf at eye level. Small and large, pink, green, red and black, they gleam in the overhead lamplight. Some stand on their own like sculptures, but others are too spongy or large to balance upright and they sit on stands specially made to hold them.

The next shelf holds many differently shaped bottles of lubes and oils. I quickly scan some of the labels: wintergreen (that might sting or be cold), strawberry, sandalwood, attar of autumn, rose, ocean, candy cane.

Below that, I recognize a collection of sounds. Sounds are straight narrow wires—some thicker than others—of varying lengths. I know they are meant to be pushed into the hole of the penis. I have seen guys in porn films poke themselves there and insert the wire all the way in. They make it look like it feels good, but the sounds actually terrify me. Could I allow Nic to try one on me?

I never say never.

The room is warm from a source I cannot detect.

I take off my robe. Beneath, I wear only the silver underwear with the hole in the back. The air hits my skin but does not make me shiver.

I go to the wall with the paddles and pick the pink one. I want to know how it feels. I want to know that sting when Nic uses it on me for the first time.

Laying the pink paddle on the side of the bed, I fetch the gold plug—the one Nic requested in the letter from my box of presents—from my robe pocket and place it beside the paddle. I will insert it as soon as I lie down, but first I scan for more toys.

I pick out a cat o'nine tails. And a pair of cuffs lined with soft faux-fur.

Finally, I go to the shelf of sounds. With shaking hands I pick out the thinnest and shortest one. I'm such a coward!

I find more toys I didn't see at first. One is a narrow plug with batteries that vibrates. Another is a two-ring device that fits around the cock and balls, also battery operated.

My skin prickles at all the sensations I can imagine from these toys. So far, Nic and I have been so wrapped up in each other that about the wildest thing he does to me is spank me. Sure, I call him Daddy and he calls me Boy and Baby Boy, but we haven't had any need to explore further. We simply enjoy being locked together in hours-long lovemaking sessions that neither of us wants to end.

I gather the things I've chosen, including the vibrating rings, and line them up at the foot of the bed.

I lie down and spread my legs, inserting the gold plug into my ass. It goes in smooth since I have already prepared myself.

Then I get on my hands and knees, butt up in the air, and wait. The plug presses in all the right places. My cock is very hard.

I remain that way for a long while. I don't know how much time has passed, but I realize I cannot maintain this position all night and into the next day waiting for Nic.

I will have to endure further punishment, I guess, because at some point I know I will fall asleep.

I want, so badly, to tug on my cock. I look up at the cock cages. After a minute, I decide. Yes, I need one.

I take down a silver tube shaped one. It is a netting of wire woven in such a way that when my cock is secure it can still be seen inside the structure. There is an open hole at the end where, if I need to, I can pee while wearing it.

I sit up on my knees and take it in hand, examining it. It has two rings at the base, one for the balls, one for the cock, and these rings are adjustable leather and will hold the cage in place once fastened. This one does not link to a plug, which is fine because I already have one inside me.

I work the cage over my hard cock, pulling my shaft through the first ring, then pulling my balls through the second. I tug the leather rings as tight as I can stand it.

The cage forces my hard cock down and presses firm against my erection. I run my hands over the structure. I can't touch myself now. I can't do anything. I'm secure down there, safe from any friction except where my cock presses against the metal.

It's a strange sensation, yet I like the look. It's heavy between my legs, and makes me feel big. And needy. And naughty.

I again assume the position Nic/Santa/Daddy ordered. I imagine him having security in this room of the same sort he said he had at the Christmas tree. Tiny hidden cameras. Spy eyes. Watching me.

I want to be good for Nic, and naughty at the same time. If I focus on the idea that he can see me from afar, I can withstand the position for a long time.

But after some hours, naturally, eventually, I fall asleep.

# 2.

## *Nic*

It has been a long night. Starry. Stormy. Rainy. Cloudy. Freezing.

The reindeer are all back in their pens feasting on sweets and fresh grain and alfalfa. They get whatever they want after each ride on Christmas Eve.

Heck, who am I kidding? They get whatever they want every single day of the year.

I should be exhausted, but after every Christmas Eve I arrive home hyper and alert. It's very difficult for me to fall to sleep after my long night of work.

And today, well, today is even more special. For I have a lover awaiting me. And not just any lover. My naughty boy. My sweet sweet baby.

Angelbaby is my forever mate. We have both been aware of this ever since I gave him the snowflake ring.

Though we have been together only one month, I know he has wondered for a while now about the differences between us. It's an unspoken truth we harbor, like that last little bit of fear you cling to as your commitment to another becomes a lifelong promise. This all-consuming difference between us is that I am immortal while he is mortal.

I've been working on that little problem with one of the most difficult spells I've ever tried to manage. By tomorrow, he'll truly know my commitment to him is final.

As I enter the foyer of my ice castle, the glimmer of Christmas decorations everywhere nearly blinds me. I have gone a bit overboard this year, I admit, but I cannot control myself where Christmas is concerned. I have even less control where Angelbaby is concerned. I want him all the time. In every way imaginable. I want to feel him, skin to skin, twenty-four hours a day every day.

That's not possible, but it's what my body and mind want. I am hopeless. I am his, and he is mine.

Wist greets me as I come through the castle door, and takes my coat, hat and scarf.

"A good job tonight, sir?" he asks.

"It went perfectly," I reply. Then I let out a big laugh that sounds like ho-ho-ho. This is something I can't always control, and long ago I gave up trying. I have a unique laugh and that's that.

I smell wonderful cooking scents from the kitchen, but I shake my head at his raised eyebrows.

Wist smiles as if he understands. All he says as he turns away is, "He's waiting for you."

I have to force myself not to run up my winding staircase to the second floor. But still, I find myself down the hall.

I go straight to my Toy Room.

I already know my boy is waiting for me. I watched him through tiny cameras as he got ready for me in that room. I watched him explore and dress himself up. I know he's even used one of my cock cages.

I have been a collector my whole life. Among many things, I collect adult toys because of my fantasies, but I have never actually used them for much. Sure, I've tried a few things on myself, but after you get as old as I am, it stops being fun all alone.

But to have another willing person to join with me in this sort of play is a dream come true for me.

I open the door to the Toy Room, which Angel left unlocked. Softly, I enter and lock the door behind me.

Angel is asleep on the bed on top of the red covers and wearing the silver panties I asked him to don. They are cut away in the back and I can see the sweet, firm curves of his ass poking up a bit. I can't see the plug. Yet.

He has one leg bent, the other straight out, and sleeps half on his side, half on his stomach, one arm clutching a pillow. His blond, unruly hair spills like rippled light across a second white pillow under his head.

Beautiful.

I walk toward the bed, keeping quiet so as not to wake him.

I see the toys he has laid out at the foot of the bed. The pink paddle with the holes in it. The fur-lined cuffs. The vibrating rings.

140

And something else I did not see on camera and that surprises me. One of my sounds.

My brave boy. He is never one to shy away from new things.

I walk around the bed toward the head and look at him, at his sweet sleeping face and pale pink lips slightly pursed, his naked shoulders bent to clutch the pillow, his hip curved and the underwear pushed down a bit because of the cock cage.

There are too many shadows between his legs to see clearly, but I can make out a glint of metal. The underwear has been tugged down just far enough to allow that cage to poke out and, hopefully, his balls.

Already I am aroused.

I reach up to his face and stroke back his hair, combing the softness between my fingers. On the third stroke, he jerks his head a little and his body stretches as he wakens. He rolls slightly back and the entire front of his body is revealed to me. The cock cage bounces up a little. So pretty. So shiny for me. Glittering in the light. The underwear is just as I imagined, pushed down under his balls. The balls bulge beneath the wire cage, held taught by a tight ring. They are dark pink and hairless, smooth from being drawn so tight, just as I like them.

My cock plumps up to full hardness beneath my red Santa pants as I gaze upon the beauty that is my baby boy.

Angel's eyes open, dark and dreamy. "Daddy?"

"Yes. I'm back. And look at you, my sweet boy."

Suddenly, Angel jumps up a little. "Oh, I'm sorry, I fell asleep! I'm so so sorry!"

Before I can utter one more word, he gets onto his hands and knees, bows his head between his shoulders and sticks his pretty ass in the air.

"I'm ready for you. I'm so ready for you. I have been waiting," he says.

"You have indeed," I reply.

Now I can see the gold plug in him. The faceted red jewel peeks up at me. It's gorgeous against his skin, and the way it winks it is as if his ass is beckoning to me.

"But I was naughty, too, Daddy." He half-whispers into the pillow.

"I know you were. You opened your gifts before you were supposed to."

"I had to peek, Daddy. I couldn't stand waiting any longer."

"But you disobeyed me. And you also disobeyed my orders in my letter to you."

"Yes, Daddy, I'm sorry I fell asleep. I was just very tired."

"I can forgive you for sleeping. I was gone for quite a while. But opening your presents before Christmas without permission? Peeking at the surprises I had for you? That's very naughty."

His backside wiggles. "I know."

I pick up the pink paddle. "I think you need a spanking. I have this pink paddle that should do the job nicely."

"Yes, sir, Daddy, sir."

There is no fear in his voice. He sticks his ass up as high as he can and braces himself on his elbows, waiting, asking, practically begging me in his body language to use the paddle.

So far, I've only ever used my hands to spank him. This will feel different to him. This will sting more.

"Are you sure you are ready, baby?" I ask.

"Yes, sir, please, Daddy. I'm prepared to take my punishment as I must."

I start to raise the paddle, but Angel lifts his head. "Daddy?"

"Yes?"

"I deserve this. Don't stop until you know it's right."

"Oh baby boy." I can feel my cock jerk at his words. I lift the paddle and smack him on one cheek.

Angel's body tenses but he remains silent. Immediately, the skin pinks, and where the holes in the paddle strike are little white dots.

I raise the paddle and strike again on the other side. The silver underwear is drawn tight, outlining his ass, making a perfect gilt frame for his loveliness.

His ass pinks up as I paddle it with sharp, quick strikes eight more times.

The way Angel holds himself, and the perkiness of his buttocks so red now, makes me feel as if am imminently close to coming. I love my boy's ass so much. The way the cheeks curve up to dimple at the lower back, the way the soft skin ripples with each strike. How Angel bears it so bravely always impresses me.

142

I put the paddle down. I hear Angel breathing in and out, not hissing, but more huffing. His body is tense but still. He has said nothing. But I know him well enough now to tell he is quite excited. The cock cage must be nearly overwhelming to him.

I run my hands gently over his reddened buttocks. He draws in a sharp breath.

"Too much?" I ask.

"N—No, Daddy."

I let out a single laugh. "You are perfect, baby boy. You handled that so well."

"Thank you, Daddy." He says the last syllable of the word daddy with a slight groan in his voice.

I move over him and gather him into my arms. He turns into me, his arms coming up and around me. His cock cage bumps my thigh, then presses between my legs.

I lay him down beneath me and lean up so I can run my hands up and down his body. I rub softly at his hard nipples until they are nubbins. I caress his ribs, stomach and waist. I dip my fingers along the insides of his thighs. He spreads his legs and groans.

I cup the rigid sac beneath the cock cage and gently squeeze. It's the softest skin of his body, smooth when pulled tight, and his balls protrude within the sac, drawing the skin even tighter.

"Such a good, boy. Such a beautiful boy," I praise.

"Oh, Daddy. That feels good." He pulls his legs up and back, showing me the crack of his ass, and there's that red stone again, flashing.

I reach down and touch it, running my finger over it, pushing on it a little. He moans.

I grab the base and pull it out to the tip, then shove it back in.

"Oh, oh, Daddy!"

"You need to take it, baby. All right? Because something bigger is coming and you need to be prepared."

"Yes, Daddy, oh yes! I can take it."

"Good boy."

I play with him like that, shoving the plug in and out of him. His hole is relaxed and loose, easily opening and closing around the ridges of the toy, sucking at it, wanting more. It's glorious to watch him take it.

I remove the plug and Angel's mouth opens. "Daddy, no. I want it back."

"It's okay. Just be patient, baby. I've got something a lot better."

I pet the cock cage and watch it jump a little. He groans.

I can't wait any longer. I can feel a dampness of my own in my underwear.

I remove my shirt as Angel gazes at me. His eyes are big as he watches me take down my Santa pants, underwear and all, to reveal my full erection. He licks his lips.

I am so ready for him, but I can't resist giving him a taste. I move forward, straddling his waist, and hold my cock to his lips. "Open."

He opens his mouth and I insert the tip. My cock is dripping, He drinks it down, sucking on the tip and moaning around it, the vibration nearly my undoing.

"I can't last if you keep doing that, baby. Just a taste, okay?"

He nods, but sucks harder.

"Bad, baby!" I pull out, the tip nearly a dark purple. I'm so close. Too close. But it's all right. We can go as long as we want, as many times as we want. The new year is coming and I'm finished until next Christmas Eve.

He gives me a look that is a combination pout and smirk when I forbid him any more suckling..

"Baby, I need to put this in you. I need to fuck you, okay? You need to let me."

"Yes, Daddy Santa, yes. You need to come inside me."

"Oh baby." His words nearly make me come right then and there.

I move down between his thighs. He holds his legs up and back again, his hole still big and loose, waiting to be filled.

I steer myself right into him and he's so oiled and stretched it's a smooth and steady slide. He's tight and hot, and I can't help but start fucking immediately, not even letting him have time to get used to me.

He does not show any sign of unease. He's been well-prepared. He's been waiting for hours. I can safely have my way with him.

Angel starts talking. "Oh Daddy, it's big. So big. I love it. Go fast. Faster. All the way in and out. Please!"

144

He has such a dirty little mouth. The cock cage jerks up and down. I used one on myself once, alone, but didn't like it much.

"Baby, does it hurt to have your cock caged like that?"

"It's heavy, Daddy, but—oh! Keep going. Please. I love it."

His muscles clench around me and I can't hold back. Three more thrusts and I'm yelling into the air. My cock throbs, releases, throbs.

"Yes, Daddy! Fill me up!"

I collapse onto him to embrace him, to kiss him, feeling the metal of the cage bite into my stomach. When I pull out and bend my knees, my cock is still dripping, still hard as stone.

After kissing Angel and getting my fill, I lean up and grasp the cage in one hand. I lean down and lick his taut ball sac.

"Oh, Daddy!"

On up close inspection, the rings look almost too tight around both balls and the base of his penis.

"This needs to be loosened," I say.

"Daddy, if you do, I'll come. I know I will!" he cries.

"Okay, baby boy. You've been good. You have my permission to come."

I loosen the rings and slide the cage off. His cock bobs into the air, the tip glistening, the shaft dark and hard. He grows now that he has room. The head points up and I lower my head.

I suck his cock into my mouth and the sweetness fills my throat.

"Daddy! Daddy!"

He erupts into my mouth. Cupping his balls, I feel the huge throb all the way from there to the back of my throat. I swallow it all. My young baby boy yells and cries out my name. "Daddy! Santa! Nic!"

He's so pent up he keeps coming for a long time before finally quieting and going limp.

I lick him clean, then draw him to my chest. He's still wearing the panties, and it's so sexy as I sit up and turn him until he is on my lap. I hug him to me and kiss his temple and cheek.

"Baby, you are so perfect."

"You are, Daddy. Better than I ever could have dreamed. Better than anything."

We rest for awhile, then do it all again. Slower this time, the spanking softer on already red buttocks, the fucking long and leisurely in all the positions we can think of.

When I have come a second time, I view Angel's hard cock with a raised eyebrow.

"Would you like to be brave?"

His lips go flat but he nods with a jerk of his head.

I pick up the sound.

He gives a gasp.

"It's all right, baby. We don't have to."

"I want to feel everything with you."

I hold the base of his cock with one hand and lick the head with the other, making him moan and squirm. I make sure I leave a lot of saliva on the tip but I still oil the sound thoroughly.

I poke the wire lightly at the head of his cock, at the tiny hole there. He gasps and holds his breath. My own cock plumps in response.

Slowly, as I hold his cock still and firm in my hand, I let the sound slip inside.

"Oh, Daddy, I don't know!"

It's in only half an inch. I stop. He's so lovely. My beautiful boy.

He breathes in, then out, then in again. "Okay."

"What does it feel like?" I ask.

"Like a tickle but scary. Because it's sort of cold. And sharp, but not sharp really. Oh! I don't know!"

"Let's try a little more. You have your safe word if you want me to stop."

He nods.

I push it into him more. His chest shudders. I go slowly until it is halfway in, and then I lick all around his head and shaft. My own cock presses fully against my belly. It's as if I haven't already come two times today.

"Oh, that feels good," my boy whines. "I want to come but it feels like something heavy is blocking me."

"Sweetheart, you're so brave. Such a good boy."

I push again. It takes time, but finally the sound is all the way in.

146

"Well?" I ask, and lean down to suck at the head of his cock and tongue the looped end of the sound.

"Oh! I like that. But it's so strange. Suck me, please. I want to feel what it's like!"

I suck the tip, lave the head, and take him halfway into my mouth.

"Oh, Daddy! Oh. It's so weird. And good, too. But I want to come. Please!"

I let his cock slip from my lips and say, "Should I take it out, then?"

"Slow, please."

I tug the loop and pull gently. The sound slides up.

"Oh," he says. "That's weird and good. Good!"

I pull a little more. It's easier coming out then going in. When it's all the way out, I suck his cock back into my mouth. He bucks into it. I stroke him and play with his hole until he comes hard.

We make love all the rest of the afternoon until we fall into an exhausted sleep.

Late into the night we leave the toy room and go downstairs to a huge feast that Wist left for us. The food is still warm under hot lamps and covered trays.

We eat mashed potatoes and macaroni and cheese. Green beans and a cold, crisp salad. We have hot buttered rolls and little toasted cheese sandwiches. Wist made a turkey of faux meat, and it tastes pretty good when you add plenty of gravy.

Dessert is pie and cake and cookies. We eat until we can't eat any more.

Then we go upstairs and back to bed.

Once we are sitting in bed in the toy room, I take Angel's face in my hands and kiss him. Light and sweet. No tongue.

"What was that for?" he asks.

"I love you."

"I love you, too, but that kiss was something... else?"

I nod. "I have been thinking ever since you moved in. Well, before that. Hours before." I smile. "When I gave you the ring in the snow."

"Yes? You want to marry me or something?" He tilts his head, his lips pressed in a tight cocky smile.

"Or something," I reply.

"My answer is yes." He grins up at me.

"Oh, baby. You know I want to marry you. You should have no question as to our love for each other."

"Daddy! I'm so happy!"

I hug him hard.

When he lets go, I cup his face in my palms again. "What I want to talk about right now, though, is about how we're different. You and I."

His eyes darken. The smile leaves his face. "It's the fact that I'm human."

I nod.

"I know," he begins. "It's not normal for you. I—I--"

"Shh." I put my finger over his lips.

"But—but Daddy, you are immortal, right?"

"Yes. And I hate the thought that we might not grow in our love forever together."

"I'm sorry--"

"Shh. No. It's not that, baby. You don't have to be sorry. This is about something I've been working on. A spell."

"A spell? For me?"

I nod.

His gaze brightens.

"Sweet baby boy, give me your ring."

He lifts his hand with the glowing sapphires on it in the shapes of snowflakes. I take the band and slide it off his finger.

"I have been working quite hard on this spell. It's the best I can do for now. But I want you to watch."

"Okay."

I take the ring between my palms and rub them together. As I do, I feel the metal heat and sparkles like fairy glitter cloud over my hands.

"Oh! Wow!" He sits up. "Daddy!"

"It's magic, Baby. But I hope it's enough magic."

When the cloud of glitter settles all over the bed, I hold out the ring. "Your hand," I say.

He lifts his left hand.

I slip the band on his ring finger. "Feel anything?" I ask.

"It's warm and it tingles a little."

I nod. "If you keep that ring on always and never take it off, you won't grow old and you won't die. It's the best I can do. For now. It will work. But only if you keep that ring on."

"Oh!" He looks down at it, touching the band with his other hand. "Oh. Daddy. That's just—oh. I have no words."

I draw him to my chest. I hold him tight as the tears fall.

"It's the most amazing gift. I still often think I'm dreaming," he says after awhile. "I don't even know what it's like to be immortal. I can't fathom it."

"Few can or ever have. But I have books about it. We'll learn together. About what sort of elf I am. About how we will walk hand in hand into the millenniums.We can read those books and study about it together."

"I would love that," Angel says.

"Good." I pull the covers over our bodies and hold Angel tight. "Go to sleep now. You'll need your energy because when we wake, I intend to take you again. And again."

"Yes, please, Daddy." He pillows his head on my chest. He holds his hand up and stares at the ring.

"I will keep this ring always," Angel says. "I promise. I won't ever take it off. I won't ever lose it. I promise, Daddy."

"I know you will, my baby. My good boy. I know you will."

"I love you so much!" He presses a kiss to the center of my chest.

"I love you, too."

My sweet boy. My baby boy. My naughty boy. Mine forever.

THE END

# Author Note

Thanks for reading!

This book, **Santa's Naughty Boy**, is part of a series of 3 standalone books set in the same universe. Each book takes place in a world where Santa and Santa's Village is real.

The first is **The Elves of Christmas**. It is a little love story of two elves who work in Santa's Workshop.

The second is **Santa's Reindeer Shifters** which is the only omegaverse story in the group, and involves fated mates between Dasher and an elf who both learn what it is to be something called an omega and an alpha in a world where those sorts of beings are very rare.

The third is, of course, the book you just read, featuring Santa and a human and a daddy/boy trope.

You can check them all out on my Amazon author page.

Readers are very welcome to come hang out with me on Facebook where I share about my works in progress, sexy teasers and humorous details about my writing process at Wendyland.

You can also join my newsletter for updates.

# ALSO BY WENDY RATHBONE

**The Kingdom of Slaves Series** (contemporary fantasy mm romance)

The Slave Palace
The Slave Harem
Master of Halloween (short story)

**The Omega Misfits** (Omegaverse mm romance)

Trust No Alpha
The Alpha's Fake Mate
Alpha's Embrace
Single Omega Dad
Omega Chattel
Omega Untamed
Alpha Daddy (novella)
Alpha Snowed In (holiday novella)

**The Imposter Series** (fantasy mm romance)

The Imposter Prince
The Imposter King

**The Moonling Prince Series** (fantasy, sci fi mm romance)

The Moonling Prince
The Coming of the Light

**The Foundling Series** (contemporary billionaire mm romance trilogy)

Rescue Me
Sacrifice Me
Remember Me

**The Fantastic Immortals Series** (fantasy/myth mm romance)

Ganymede: Abducted by the Gods
Zeus: Conquering his Heart

## Stand Alone Novels

*Sci Fi MM Romance*

Solstice Gift (holiday)
Not Another Hero
Cocky Virgin Prince
Prey
Scoundrel
The Android and the Thief (Second edition)
Letters to an Android

*Fantasy MM Romance*

Lord Vampyre
Lace (vampire fairies)
Snow of the White Hills (mm fairy tale)
The Elves of Christmas (holiday magical)
Santa's Reindeer Shifters (holiday magical mpreg omegaverse)
Santa's Naughty Boy (holiday magical daddy/boy)

*Contemporary MM Romance*

Romantically Incorrect
Snowfall and Romance (Christmas/holiday)
The Bodyguard's Valentine
Buying You

# WENDY RATHBONE'S TROPE CHEAT SHEET

**Omegaverse non-shifter:**
Trust No Alpha, The Alpha's Fake Mate, Alpha's Embrace, Single Omega Dad, Omega Chattel, Omega Untamed, Alpha Daddy, Alpha Snowed In

**Omegaverse shifter:**
Santa's Reindeer Shifters

**Daddy kink:**
Alpha Daddy, Omega Untamed (light), Santa's Naughty Boy

**Master/slave, indentured servant:**
The Slave Palace, The Slave Harem, Scoundrel, The Android and the Thief, Letters to an Android, Prey, Solstice Gift, Ganymede, The Imposter Prince

**Captive rescue:**
Trust No Alpha, Alpha's Embrace, Omega Chattel, The Imposter Prince, The Imposter King, The Foundling Trilogy (Rescue Me, Sacrifice Me, Remember Me), Ganymede, Zeus, Prey, Scoundrel, The Android and the Thief, Letters to an Android, Lace, Snow of the White Hills

**Single dad:**
Single Omega Dad

**Fated mates:**
The Omega Misfits series, Lace, Santa's Reindeer Shifters

**Gay Harem:**
The Slave Harem

**Fake identity, fake mate:**

The Alpha's Fake Mate, The Imposter Prince, The Imposter King, Not Another Hero

**Hurt/comfort, healing:**
The Kingdom of Slaves series, The Omega Misfits series, The Imposter series, The Moonling Prince series, The Foundling trilogy, Zeus, Prey, Lace, Snow of the White Hills,

**Mafia, underworld kingpin:**
The Foundling trilogy

**Vampires:**
Lace, Lord Vampyre

**Friends to Lovers:**
Cocky Virgin Prince, Letters to an Android, The Android and the Thief

**Famous, model, actor:**
Buying You, Romantically Incorrect, Not Another Hero

**MMM scenes:**
Lace, Lord Vampyre, The Slave Harem

**First time, virgin:**
The Slave Palace, Trust No Alpha, The Alpha's Fake Mate, Alpha's Embrace, Omega Chattel, Alpha Daddy, The Imposter Prince, The Moonling Prince, Cocky Virgin Prince, Ganymede, Zeus, Not Another Hero, Prey, The Android and the Thief, Letters to an Android, Lace, Lord Vampyre, Snow of the White Hills, Santa's Reindeer Shifters

# SANTA'S REINDEER SHIFTERS
**Wendy Rathbone**

'Twas the week before Christmas,
the elves were all stressed
with Santa's lead reindeer
not feeling his best.

Something is wrong with Dasher. He's not eating. He's listless.

Silver, a stable boy elf in Santa's Village, watches over Dasher to make sure his condition does not worsen. One night, Dasher vanishes and a naked young elf is sitting in his place.

Silver has never been more attracted to anyone in his life. As he helps Dasher keep all of this a secret and hide him in his cabin, feelings between them ignite.

But Silver has a duty to Dasher to help him regain his reindeer form and make sure he flies on Christmas Eve. It might mean losing Dasher forever.

This fantasy shifter-omegaverse tale is about two fated mates who risk their jobs, their livelihoods, and Santa's rules to be together.

First time shifter, m/m omegaverse, virgin, heat/rut, fated mates, mpreg, the North Pole, Santa's Village, Christmas miracles, HEA.

# THE ELVES OF CHRISTMAS
## Wendy Rathbone

Two months before Christmas at the North Pole, Santa's workshop bustles with activity. Santa is coming early with only half a day's warning to inspect the elves' progress!

Pepper, who designs and makes special one-of-a-kind dolls, is ordered by his boss Jingle to take time out of toy-making to wash three stories of windows and decorate every room in preparation for Santa. He assigns Ice to assist. But for Pepper, it's a bit of a problem. Ice is a surly elf, even disrespectful toward Santa, while Pepper reveres Santa to the point of hero-worship. An unlikely pairing, they must work together in order to finish before Santa's arrival.

But can two elves with conflicting value systems even get along?

Amidst secrets, resentments, toasted cheese sandwiches, snowman building, a blizzard, and Santa's nerve-wracking visit, Pepper and Ice discover a mutual attraction. If they can overcome wrongful assumptions and failed expectations, love might just take its natural course and lead them to a Merry Christmas.

# OMEGA UNTAMED
## The Omega Misfits Book 6
## Wendy Rathbone

Kee is a beautiful Omega and popular rent boy living in a part of Old Town called the Trenches. He's also an untamable addict. Wild and troubled, Kee is kidnapped by Alpha drug lords who think he knows too much.

Trapped, Kee longs for a way out of the hole he's dug for himself...but who would rescue a crazy Omega sex worker?

One Alpha will. His name is Bast. Bast knows he can't tame Kee through kindness, but he still wants him for his very own.

Kee needs an Alpha who will take control, hold him down, keep him from the worst of himself. Turns out, Bast is the very man for the job.

Non-shifter omegaverse, mpreg, rescue, an uninhibited Omega, a tough Alpha with a heart of gold, daddy care, bonding/knotting and HEA.

# SINGLE OMEGA DAD
## The Omega Misfits Book 4
### Wendy Rathbone

My new financial guardian, Mathias, is a cold, self-centered, rude-ass Alpha and the son of one of the wealthiest men in the country. To him, I am a burden on society, only fit to live on a chattel farm.

It doesn't matter that I'm drawn to him, to his ominous presence and chiseled jaw, his muscular body in his fitted silk suits. I'm a single dad with kids and responsibilities --I don't have time for that rich bastard.

He keeps coming by the house so I can sign documents, fine. But then he's got cute gifts for my kids.

It's got to stop. I don't have time to fix him. Don't have time to fall in love with an Alpha right now.

A non-shifter Alpha/Omega love story with mpreg, a single widower Omega dad, an Alpha who cannot knot, emotional issues, two adorable identical twin boys, and an HEA.

Some characters from "Trust No Alpha" make appearances in this novel, however, this book is a standalone read.

# TRUST NO ALPHA
## The Omega Misfits, Book 1
### Wendy Rathbone

It's a world gone mad. The Alphas are out of control. When you discover you're not who you thought you were, the nightmare begins.

KRIS
At age eighteen, life as he knows it is over for Kris. A secret to his nature he was not aware of has been revealed.

Now, kept as a prisoner in a locked room in the mansion of his wealthy father, Kris is at the mercy of Alpha laws and Alpha domination.

Things take a turn for the worse when his own litter mate threatens him, and his father starts behaving strangely around him.

Escape is his only hope. But where can he go in a world that allows him no rights?

THORNE
Marked as a dangerous Alpha, and living a secluded life alone and unloved, Thorne still grieves for the mate whose death he feels responsible for.

Years have passed, and he refuses to even try to function in normal society.

One day he discovers a young man on his property, disheveled, desperate, and scared. He acts like a runaway Omega, but he doesn't smell like one.

What is this boy? And why does Thorne feel an immediate need to protect him? To bond him? To make him his?

A non-shifter, Omegaverse love story of rescue, first time, fertility issues and an HEA. Standalone read. 65,500 words. (While Omegas are birth-fathers in this universe, there is no on-page mpreg in this book.)

# THE ALPHA'S FAKE MATE
## The Omega Misfits, Book 2
### Wendy Rathbone

The Alphas think they own everything. Including people. Well, I'm here to say they don't own me, and I will never let one of those bastards touch me again.

The frenzy of their Burn cannot be trusted. I know from experience. My first time with an Alpha nearly ended in my death. And because of the laws which favor Alpha rights, and place a large number of unbonded, adult Omegas on chattel farms, my abuser can never be tried for his crimes against me.

Omegas are being hurt. Omegas are dying.

All Alphas are violent. Or so I believe. Until I meet Orion.

Ori is everything a guy could want in a mate. Six foot three. Beautiful brown wavy hair. Bright, dark eyes. Muscles like chiseled marble. He even says "please" and "thank you" at all the right times. He's got it all, except he's an Alpha.

Though he has given me a room in his home free of charge, and has signed fake paperwork saying we are bonded so I don't have to answer my attacker's claim, can I trust him?

But now I'm in danger. If I don't take a real mate, my life as I know it will be over. Can I believe in the goodness of Ori? Can I learn to love again?

A non-shifter, fake mate, Alpha/Omega love story. Rescue. First time. Omegaverse. Mpreg. Healing from sexual trauma. (All books in The Omega Misfits series are standalone reads and can be read in any order.) 61k words.

# OMEGA CHATTEL
## The Omega Misfits Book 5
**Wendy Rathbone**

At Zilly's Chattel Farm, Alli is seen as an upstart Omega. But in reality, he is the victim of a brutal house-dad who wants to control him. Threatened with being institutionalized when he turns eighteen, Alli runs away.

Tarin is an Alpha who runs a small school from his own home for wayward Omegas. Three or four students at a time are all he can handle and his home is full. But when he meets Alli on the streets, he is compelled to bring him home.

Alli wants a better future for himself, better than selling himself on the streets, so he agrees to be a student, when what he really wants is Tarin himself. Tarin doesn't sleep with his Omega students, and the one exception he made broke his heart.

But Alli is persistent. And not only does Tarin have a weakness for broken young men, there seems to be a spontaneous bond forming between them. The combination is turning hotter faster than they can keep up.

Non-shifter omegaverse, fated mates, mpreg, age gap, virgin, knotting/bonding, high steam, HEA.

# ALPHA'S EMBRACE
**The Omega Misfits Book 3**
**Wendy Rathbone**

I am Misha. My name was given to me at birth by the doctor who delivered me. I have never known my parents. I live in a ten by ten space with one window, a sink and toilet, a bed and a locked door. Once a day I'm taken to an outdoor exercise area. I am allowed a limited access tablet and tutored online by computer programs. I have one friend I talk to through a tiny crack in the wall. His name is Cedric and he has trouble keeping himself quiet. When he isn't talking to me about monsters and demons, he screams all the time.

Why is my life so isolated and depressing? Because I am a Sylph. Sylphs are the byproduct of illegal Omega to Omega matings. We are all beautiful, but 99.9% are born insane. The rarest of Sylphs, like me, show no outward signs of madness or brain damage, but we live in institutions because we cannot be trusted.

All of us Sylphs who have lived long enough to pass through puberty have hypersexual disorder which makes life even more difficult for us, let alone our keepers. It is like something Alphas call the Burn, a mating urge Alphas experience once every couple of months.

But we're Sylphs, not Alphas, and this Burn thing? We experience it all the time. It's a huge problem and why we are kept isolated. Most of us don't survive through our teens because of it.

One day, a handsome Alpha comes to interview and study me. He calls himself the Chief of Staff but his real name is Geo. Like magic, I fall in love with him instantly. I do everything I can to seduce him. He will have none of it because touch between an Alpha and a Sylph is taboo. But I have plans. No matter what, I intend to bond him and make him mine. Forever.

A non-shifter Alpha/Omega-Sylph love story of forbidden love, rescue, and HEA. Standalone read. No Mpreg. 58k words

# SONS OF NEVERLAND
## *A Deliciously Dark Male/Male Romance*
# Della Van Hise

Set against a backdrop of contemporary culture, *Sons of Neverland* explores the universal questions of love, sex and death - the three most crucial challenges every human being must face. Stefan London is a grieving man, suffering through the loss of his young daughter. When he goes to a science fiction convention in the hopes of meeting her friends, he encounters instead a man who is dangerously seductive. Lured into the night, Stefan soon discovers himself in a world where vampires are real, and immortality is only a kiss away.

But the price of eternal life is high, and as his handsome maker warns, "Through my blood you will learn a secret that will compel you to live forever, yet a secret so sinister it will haunt you for that same eternity."

The secret will haunt you, too.

———

*A deliciously dark male/male romance. First time, enemies to lovers, love/hate relationship, HEA.*

## YEAR OF THE RAM
## Della Van Hise

*Year of the Ram* was described by one reviewer as... "A space-faring gay romance full of love, angst, and longing."

Only after Star Commander Morgan Diego becomes an exile as a result of a Galaxy Corps political blunder does he begin to realize how much he valued the companionship of his second in command - the mysterious Lucien, an Alfarian who is more elfen than human, with peculiar powers & abilities which begin to unfold as he, too, realizes what he has lost.

Separated by circumstance from his former life, Morgan is thrust into a world where he must survive by his wits. When he meets a peculiar little old man calling himself Kim Le, Morgan finds himself in a situation where he is required to master The Art - not only a form of human & extraterrestrial martial arts, but a way of living that will alter his life forever.

At the temple, he is introduced to his new teacher, another Alfarian man who begins to steal his heart - a heart which is already promised to Lucien. Torn and conflicted, Morgan struggles with the world he left behind and the world he now inhabits.

Beginning to believe he may never again return to his ship and to the friends and loved ones he left behind, he is all the more frustrated and heartbroken when a new Master arrives at the temple: a man to whom Morgan is immediately drawn both mentally and physically, a man who is strikingly familiar... yet utterly alien.

*M/M and M/M/M. An epic love story with a HEA.*